The Ghost On Number 2

By

Richard J. Domann

Jason
Enjoy the ghost!
she gives a good
whack!
Dick

This book is a work of fiction. Places, events, and situations in this story are purely fictional. Any resemblance to actual persons, living or dead, is coincidental.

ISBN: 1-4140-0629-2 (e-book)
ISBN: 1-4140-0630-6 (Paperback)

Library of Congress Control Number: 2003096960

This book is printed on acid free paper.

Printed in the United States of America
Bloomington, IN

1stBooks - rev. 10/30/03

One

I wished that I would just heave my guts out and get it over with. But no, my physical system seemed to cherish the residual alcohol it still held onto. Complete with all the unique negative side effects. The bright blue North Carolina morning did nothing for my raging headache. It was Monday, mid-August and as I drove down I-40 towards work, I realized the scary fact that my alcohol tolerance had progressed to the point where I could function pretty well even though I was sporting a major league hang over. My sorry situation was, I thought, worth the price. The day before, a perfect late summer Sunday, I had been strolling down the legendary fairways of the Number 2 course at The Pinehurst Country Club in Pinehurst, NC. The dream round that I was living had a surreal air to it. This had been my first time playing the Number 2 course. I had the opportunity to visit as a spectator on several occasions. The first time I set foot on No. 2 was shortly after I moved my family down to North Carolina from Wisconsin. The golf occasion was the 1990 Tournament Players Championship. My wife Mary, our two young boys, Eric and Josh, and I wanted to see the pros play. We patiently waited to find a vantage point where the kids could see clearly. We found a spot along the right side of the par three seventeenth hole. Mary and I were getting a kick out of the boys, who were peeking their young blonde heads through the legs of extremely tolerant observers. They were trying to get a better look at the pros who slashed away at the little white golf balls in that year's Tournament Players Championship. Our offspring had just wedged themselves into a perfect spot when the tour's current superstar, Greg Norman, after executing a beautiful shot on number 17, bent down, smiled and gave them each a souvenir ball as he walked past. I had a feeling right then and there that Pinehurst No. 2 held some special magic for me and for my family. Little did I know how prophetic this thought would become. The second time we visited, again as a family unit, we all caught our first glimpse of the legendary Jack Nicklaus as he teed it up for the 1994 Senior United States Open. I virtually dragged my young boys up the path towards the huge scoreboard in front of the practice tee and got us all in a position to stand in the rarified air of the greatest golfer of all time. That Senior Open was won by Simon Hobday, who after stumbling up the eighteenth, desperately sought a cold glass of beer. The smile on his victorious face was a sight all golf fans appreciated. One of the "good guys" had won the Open. My whole family, and the friends that went to the tournament with us, thought it was nice to see up close that the seniors not only still had the fire of competition in their bellies, but that they truly enjoyed the fans who came to see them play as well. We had seen the Bear in person. And we had seen a great championship. Pinehurst still held the magic for us. The last time, prior to my playing there, was bittersweet in that I was now alone. I walked past the bronze statues of Donald Ross and Richard Tufts and should have been at peace. Unfortunately I was miserable. But through my veil of personal blue I was to experience what many golf addicts felt was the greatest U.S. Open ever played. The 99th U.S. Open Championship held during June of 1999.

Payne Stewart's 72nd hole heroics over Phil Mickelson marked another milestone in his glittering career and another stumble in Phil's. The event was truly "one moment in time" made even more poignant by Stewart's sudden death less than a year later. His final fateful airplane flight cast a mourning wreath over the world of golf, but the tragedy may have succeeded in elevating Stewart's already established "tour star" status to the level of legend. Those previous visits to Pinehurst No. 2 had set up my anticipation for actually playing the course myself. It had been a great day, but oh what a hangover. Even through my blur the memory of playing No. 2 brought back feelings of sheer delight. From the bull shoulders of the elderly caddie named Eddie, who looped my bag around Donald Ross' masterpiece, to his tactful advice, which earned me a smooth 75. Without Eddie mumbling pointed little comments like, "*better aim more to da left*

Misser W", which came to my ears most often on the inverted saucer-shape Donald Ross greens, my putt total would have sent my score well into the mid-eighties. After we finished playing, our group sat down to a victory dinner in the old hotel's Carolina Room and a post-round celebration in the Ryder Cup Lounge. The Sunday night party with my playing partners had nearly done me in this morning, but I was supposed to have a light day at the office. I figured that I was going to make it.

Two

I knew I could push my way through the day until the residual alcohol in my system worked its way out of me. The four-story parking deck at work was packed, but I finally found a spot. I slid my BMW Z3 into its proper slot and walked into the glass encased office structure bearing the name *Cattigan Building*. This was the seat of power of Quantest Inc. leader in pharmaceutical testing and biotechnology innovation. The Cattigan Building, one of fifteen on the Quantest campus held eight hundred fifty nine employees and was dubbed the companies' Western Hemisphere headquarters. QI, as it had become known to industry personnel had the quickest uptake of any of the fast growing biotech-testing firm on the eastern seaboard. As a hot company, QI was growing fast and we were all looking forward to even greater international opportunities through mergers and acquisitions. But that was still a few years off. The fledgling new firm had started out as a small group of ten disgruntled scientists. They were all cast off from a big pharma company, Thor Inc., following a hostile takeover. QI had grown quickly based on the reputation of these ten men and women. They were smart. They were honest. And they were accurate. In the pharmaceutical testing business those three characteristics were everything. If your company ever lost one of those traits it was done. I pictured their faces, one by one, and felt a great sense of pride. This business needs integrity. One slip and you were out of the game just as fast as you got into it. The biotechnology side of the business had not fully developed yet, but it held great promise. The ten original employees of Quantest dubbed themselves the Foreign Legion. And they acted like it. None of the premier Wall Street analysts would have, or could have, figured a small group of scientists would bind together and ruthlessly begin a campaign of acquisition, domination and practical success by measuring products in a field that only had a handful of marketable brands. But that is exactly what they did. They built the company fast and they built it good. Many more stars from the pharmaceutical industry liked what they saw and came to join up. The next generation of Legionnaires was on the move. I was one of the best of this next wave. I brought with me from one of the largest of the big pharmaceutical companies, Manna Pharmaceuticals Inc., a record of achievement in sales and marketing that few had ever seen. I was destined to hit the top at Manna. Then, when poised to make my move up the executive ladder, my family life began to crumble and the tumble began. I still had all the tools to compete in the big pharma business world, but something critical was lacking. My superiors at Manna began to look past me, and just as I began to slip into middle management obscurity a recruiter called with an offer from Quantest Inc.

QI didn't care what Manna thought I was lacking. In this highly competitive industry, when the opportunity to bring talent like me, on board the team at QI made sure that they got me. I grossed a huge salary in the process and pocketed untold numbers of stock options. So at the ripe young age of 44, and in spite of whatever personal demons I was battling within myself, I looked like the picture of success. That past history always seemed to rear its ugly head each time I walked the tile steps to the building where my office was housed. Armed to face another day in the corporate jungle, even with a mind-blunting hangover, I pushed open the glass revolving door to the Cattigan Building. This Monday morning, hung over but glowing after a round of golf at Pinehurst, I presented a strange contrast to the man whom for the past several months had been wallowing in personal self-doubt and pity.

Three

"Hello, Mr. Wolters," Sakina, one of the newly hired security officers, said to me sweetly. "How was your weekend?"

"Same as always Sakina. I missed shooting my age again by 26 strokes. I don't think I'm ever going to make it." I was going to leave it at that, but I couldn't walk away without bragging a little bit. "Just kidding. I had a great day down at Pinehurst yesterday. I brought No. 2 to its knees." Sakina nodded in appreciation and smiled.

"No. 2…I take it that's a golf course?"

"Yeah, kiddo. But it's not a golf course. It's ***the*** golf course." I said emphasizing the

THE. My head still throbbed, but I was able to put on a good show as I lingered at the front desk. I thought briefly about my shrink, Dr. LaFleur. What would she have to say about me coming to work hung over again? It was one of the many guilt trips she laid on me while she was trying to get me to face my current personal situation. I knocked her out of my head and focused back on Sakina. This young girl was well worth noticing. I tried not to stare too much as I moved on down the hallway. Sakina laughed at my comment as I walked past her desk. She shook her braids gently. She was a beautiful dark skinned girl with a dazzling personality. She would have many young tar heels running after her over in Chapel Hill I was certain. "Keep up the good work Sakina." I said. "How many more credits do you need to finish up at UNC?"

"One more year Mr. Wolters. Then I am out of here."

"Good luck. See you later." I smiled at her one more time prior to pressing the elevator button for the fifth floor. I could almost feel the heat of her gaze as she gave the once over to my backside. Several female heads turned my way as I moved through the office complex toward the upper management side of the building. Technically I was not "Upper Management" yet but most of the other employees saw which way my talents were taking me. It would not be long before I would be sitting behind a large mahogany door discussing major strategies and tactics with the original members of the Foreign Legion.

Four

"Hey Tom!" Billy Parker yelled as he scurried down the hall. My head throbbed. "Guess what? I had four birdies on Saturday and still didn't break eighty! God I stink! And I was playing with Scolcroft on top of it. I think I'm just going to give up the game. My head is never in the right place for all eighteen holes. I can get off fourteen good ones and then...BAM!" He slapped his hands right in front of my face and I thought I would drop right there. "The fricking wheels fall off!" He continued. "That's when I flip the top of the flask, let a sweet burning stream of Grand Marnier flow down my throat and march on. I'll never get this handicap down to single digits." Billy was a great guy. One of my relatively few close friends at QI. Ron Scolcroft was one of the original Foreign Legion. His expertise came from his ability to thread his way through the Gordian Knot called the FDA. Getting through the FDA approval process is never easy and sometimes can be deadly. Tradition has it that new drug applications, or NDA's as they were often called, need to be submitted in perfect condition to the Food and Drug Administration. They rarely are, not because drug company regulatory departments are incompetent, but because the FDA, full of underpaid bureaucrats, live to stall pharmaceutical company progress. This attitude was seeping over into their biotech and testing branch. QI hoped that Scolcroft could help the company miss some of the traditional hurdles. The FDA, like a lot of regulatory agencies, had a long history of conservative action when it came to new drug approvals. This attitude was initiated by some of their "best" employees. Back in the sixties one of the FDA's shining bureaucratic stars was a female researcher who had delayed approval of a heart medication from a new drug class called beta-blockers. This drug had some questionable early results, so "the FDA star" instituted some delaying tactics like asking for further studies, asking for more complete summarization of clinical protocols and so forth. The result was a delay of over seven years. FDA proclaimed that she had saved "countless" lives due to her diligence. During the years while the stall was on, the drug had been approved in Europe with no untoward, life-threatening side effects to those patients who took it. The epidemiological facts later showed that in the U.S. nearly forty thousand people with heart conditions who could have benefited from the approval of the heart medicine...died. Chalk one up for the FDA. Ron Scolcroft cut his teeth during this era and consistently fought the FDA and their conservative nature. Drugs in therapeutic areas such as diabetes, asthma and arthritis all had come to market months ahead of schedule due to his work, and his relationships. Naturally he fit right in to the Foreign Legion. His prosperity was assured as his reputation grew throughout the industry. Scolcroft still groveled with those of us in the "lower" ranks of middle management when he needed a golf game. Golf and Scolcroft were spiritually linked. Unfortunately no one liked to play with him because he was cheap. Scolcroft was renowned as a man who still had his first communion money. It amazed all of us in the up and comers, as we were dubbed, that a guy who had so much money in the bank and was making even more in the markets could be so cheap. I turned back to

Billy, smiled and thought of how much he would have had to shell out just to play in the presence of one of the heads of our company. "Don't worry Billy you will," I chuckled. "Just keep at it and work on your short game. That handicap will come down." I mopped the sweat off of my brow as I turned the knob on my modest office door. The office was pretty nice for my grade level, but I couldn't help thinking of what kind of office space I would be walking into if things had turned out at Manna. But...that was not the way to start a new week. So I shut that thought out fast. Parker hung around my office for a few more minutes bitching about his stance, his putting and lack of a good sex life and then as fast as he had come, he left. Billy really was one of my confidants at QI, but only there. I had played golf with him several times at the club, but I never considered him one of my regular golf partners. My office looked pretty much the same as it did on Friday afternoon when I had left. One stack of papers sat on the desk off in the far-left corner. Those were things I had scanned through and not acted on. A clean black blotter with some executive golf toys lined up across the top of it held today's schedule. A playable miniature replica of Number 18 at Pebble Beach stuck out as the most interesting of the toys. My phone, complete with eight extensions sat on the right. I put it close to the window so I could gaze out at a stand of loblolly pines and maybe glimpse a cardinal while talking testing price allowances and potential buy-in deals to clinics and suppliers who would be handling our product lines. Behind my desk a Dell Latitude laptop computer sat hooked up to a seventeen-inch monitor and waited for me to bring it to life and begin the work week. I sighed, clicked on the computer and walked out of the office to get a hot cup of coffee while the latest Michael Dell computer beast warmed up.

Five

In the break room I smiled when I ran into Mickey Laughlin who was spinning off two quick Clinton jokes to anyone who would listen as he poured a steaming cup of decaf into his "Rush Limbaugh is right" coffee mug. Mickey laughed louder than I did and he promised to e-mail me a few clip art shots of Hillary that he had found on some right leaning political web page. As we chuckled over the demise of the former Commander-in-Chief, which was now becoming old news, Patti Nolan, one of our co-workers, stormed into the break area and registered her disgust at the juvenile nature of two supposed grown up businessmen laughing at the office of the Presidency. Being dressed down by the office liberal left wing champion was not on the agenda for either myself or Mickey who began a tirade of semi-true comments regarding the former President's personal decisions which only served to enflame Patti even more. By the end of the exchange the temperature in the break room had risen considerably. I strode back off to my waiting computer. Mickey snickered all the way back to his mid-hallway office. I could visualize Patti kicking the Coke machine with the ire of a harpy. She would be beginning slow breathing exercises as she tried to calmly pour herself a cup of Celestial Seasonings Red Rose Tea. She would succeed in calming down, and then she would vow to avoid all obnoxious conservative right wing extremists.

Six

Back in my office I sat down in front of my computer screen and began to weed through the fifteen new e-mails that had landed in my inbox. In the middle of my attempt to unzip Mickey's Hillary Clinton clip art the phone rang. I punched the small gray rectangle which had my name printed on top of it.

"Tom Wolters. Can I help you?"

"Hey Tom, its Paul. How's it going down there?" On the phone was one of our Clinical Trial Account Managers, Paul Webster. "The leaves are just turning up here but it won't be long 'til they're all gone."

"Hey Paul." I said. "Things are fine down here. What's up with you?"

"Listen, I need you to come up here next week and help me with some customers. This is really important. I got the big shots from the Thorvald Clinic to join me for eighteen holes of golf at Whistling Straits in Kohler next Saturday and then we're going to drive up to Lambeau to watch the Packers and the Bears from their corporate skybox. They're really going to put the push on me to do that experimental testing program I was telling you I pitched to them last month and I can't do this without home office support. Besides I need help with the budget on this thing." I thought to myself...here it comes. Paul continued, "Whistling Straits is about two hundred fifty bucks per person and I told them we would pay for the tailgate party before the game in Green Bay. Whadda ya say? Can you make it?"

I wiped my forehead again and quickly scanned my calendar. "Hell yes I can make it, but can I get back to North Carolina in time for a Monday afternoon meeting?" I saw time blocked off on my calendar. "Remember Preston Brough? He's leaving the company and we're having a going away bash for him. I really shouldn't miss it." Preston and I went back to our early days in the industry. He was a great friend. "He wants to have everyone who helped him along join him for a farewell splash before he leaves the company. He's been planning this thing for three weeks." Preston was going to try to set up his own company. I was certain he was going to be a success. His event is all set up at the new Wakefield TPC course. If we can we could fly in on Monday afternoon, have the group dinner at Jimmy V's Monday night, listen to Brough talk about the future of his new company Tuesday morning, and then play Wakefield Tuesday afternoon with him and the rest of the potential investors." This would be a great opportunity and I hoped Paul would see it that way too. Paul thought about it for a moment. "I'm not scheduled for anything else, so if I can work out the travel, the flight from Green Bay should be a go. Sounds like this Brough meeting is big. I don't know him that well. You sure it's ok if I tag along?" I assured him it would be ok. "Thanks," he said. "You never know when it might be time to move on again, you know." I hadn't really thought about another job change, especially with QI in such a good position, but with my personal life in a state of flux I had to be prepared for anything. "You sure we can we do Whistling Straights, Green Bay and then get back in time?"

"Let me get Theresa on it right away." Theresa was Paul's admin. "If she can book the travel right maybe we can blow out of Green Bay right after the game, get to

Milwaukee in time to catch a flight that will get us to RDU in decent enough time." Paul hesitated. "Does that work? Will it matter if you are just a little bit late?"

"Wait," I said. "Just have Theresa check on the flights first then call me back later this morning and we'll make final plans." My hangover had surged back and I had to get off the phone. "Call me back as soon as you find anything out. If I'm not in my office use my cell phone. I'll make sure I have it on." I thought about what a great trip this would be. "Paul, this sounds super. Let's hope it works out."

"It will," he said. "Talk to you soon." I hung up the phone and smiled.

Wow, I thought. This was the break I needed. Away from work. Away from home. Just another great escape in the name of business. I hit the release button on my telephone and immediately began to process how I could work this trip out. My next door neighbor Cathy would watch the kids. That was mandatory to make sure that they wouldn't have any more parties or anything. Then maybe I could fly into Milwaukee early on Thursday and catch up with some of the old gang. It had been over two years since I had seen any of them and even though we corresponded via e-mail quite frequently there was nothing like seeing them all in person. Especially during the month of October. Even though I probably wouldn't be able to get up there, it would be nearly Oktoberfest time in LaCrosse. A trip to God's Country was just what I really needed to pull out of my doldrums, but that probably wasn't going to happen. I reached into the top drawer of my desk, grabbed a yellow legal pad and began a to do list. As I jotted down a potential series of events a smooth cold shudder ran up my spine. The air conditioning was down so even though it was a bit unnerving I ignored what I later would know was a signal and kept adding to my list. I sat thinking about the trip when the phone began to purr. I wondered why no one was answering it. After five rings I picked it up and said hello. "Mr. Wolters, this is Mount Birch High School. We have your son Josh here in the office. He says he's not feeling well and wants you to come and get him."

"Okay," I said as I glanced at my watch. "I'll be there in thirty minutes."

Seven

My calendar was clean so I knew I could make the run to the school. I had been having trouble with Josh and his older brother Eric lately so I figured this would be a good bridge to an overdue father-to-son talk. I straightened up my desk, forwarded my phone and walked quickly out to the parking lot waving at Sakina as I left the building. I popped down the top of the Z3 and sped out of the QI parking lot. The low hung vehicle was a blast to drive on days like this and I relished the fact that it would take some time to pick up Josh, drop him off at home and then speed back to work with enough time to round out the rest of my Monday. My hangover was fading. I was starting to feel good again. Mount Birch High School was only two years old and was very well equipped for a public school. I could afford to send the boys to private school, but felt that they would get a better social education not being with a bunch of snotty rich kids. I wondered if I made the right choice as I sped off of Highway 55 and onto the school grounds. The student parking lot was filled with many upscale foreign cars regardless of its public school status. As I walked through the glass front doors a small mob of teens slid down the hall giggling and pushing at each other the wonderful way that only teens can do and get away with. In grade school some craggy old teacher would be yelling for them to keep their hands to themselves. In the adult world that kind of physical behavior would be unthinkable. The scene made me think back to my high school days in Granville Falls. Briefly I thought how great it was going to be to see the old gang again. I had to set my trip so that I could arrive on Thursday before the big Thorvald meeting. My friends were classics...Duck, Greek, Linda, Cheri. Cheri Wilson. One of my early crushes. Actually, the first big love. Great body, long raven hair, tight fitting bell-bottom, hip hugging jeans. I snapped back to the present and glanced around at a group of female students walking down the glossy linoleum floors of the new high school. The girls today actually dressed quite the same as they did during my high school days in the seventies. Hip hugging bell-bottoms. Midriff tops long straight hair parted down the middle. They all looked strangely familiar. I swore that I saw ghosts of Cheri, Wanda and Lynn. I shook my head and came back to the present again. The boys from this generation dressed altogether different than we did. The hair was the same as back in the seventies. Long hair was in. Hanging over the ears in sweeping waves on top of acne splotched faces. But instead of the tight button fly bell bottom jeans we wore post Viet Nam, these boys were wearing big baggy cargo pants that drooped down their butts and lagged over their shoes or sandals. Some things just seemed to go round and round. Others just passed on and got picked up in little pieces by other generations.

The attendance office was halfway down the main hall just past the cafeteria. I walked into the neat office, a plant stood in one corner, a long low couch sat opposite a tall wooden counter. Behind the counter a bleach blonde chubby woman probably in her mid-thirties smiled and asked me if she could be of help.

"Yes," I said. "My name is Tom Wolters. I came to pick up my son Josh. I was told that he wasn't feeling well." The hefty blonde's face paled noticeably. She fidgeted a bit, her feet moved back and forth. She asked me to wait one moment while she got the principal. I began to smell the unmistakable odor of trouble. The pit of my stomach lurched when I saw the face of the high school principal coming out into the front office.

"Mr. Wolters?"

"Yes," I said. "What's wrong? Where's Josh?"

"He's in the nurse's office. She is cleaning him up."

"What happened!?" I shouted, not meaning to raise my voice to the level that it had reached.

The principal ran his fingers through his short gray hair and looked at me with a mixture of pity and disgust. He said, "Don't worry. He'll be ok...

Just as soon as he sobers up."

Eight

I got Josh home and in spite of wanting to ask a series of sane, controlled questions I immediately flew off the handle. I didn't know how much he was going to remember, because he was still quite buzzed, but screaming at him seemed to do me a lot of good. I left him with one blazing thought that I felt sure his alcohol soaked brain would be able to hold on to. "Do not leave this house until I get home and we get a chance to talk about this!" I then stormed out and drove back to QI. The rest of the afternoon was a blow off for me. I sat in my office. Brooded over how my life was so radically split. My professional side was quite disciplined, solid, productive, promising. My personal side was miserably chaotic, weak, disjointed, and gloomy. I called my shrink and made an appointment for Wednesday. She told me to come in earlier. Tomorrow, if possible. The end of the day finally came and I decided to stop in at my favorite watering hole, the Painted Turtle, for a quick one before I went home to lay down the law to Josh.

Nine

My glassy eyes peered through a growing mental mist. I glanced up at a young dark haired male bartender, I thought his name was Mark, as I finished my third Grey Goose vodka on the rocks and then decided to have one more. Facing Josh could wait. Feeding the boys could wait. No one else was at the house waiting to welcome me home. I had only come in to The Turtle for a quick one, but I was way past that now. I got up to go to the Men's Room and bumped a waitress carrying a large tray. "Oh! I'm sorry Mr. Wolters. I didn't see you coming."

"Well, watch yourself," I barked as I kept walking to the restroom. "Stupid bitch." I muttered under my breath. Peter Wick, the bar manager at the club must have overheard me because he came over and asked if everything was ok.

"Yeah. No problem." I told him. "Do you need a cab Mr. W?" He asked. "No, just get me another double. I'll be back in a minute." I didn't see Peter walk over to the bar and signal the young man behind it that I was officially cut off. In the Men's Room I looked into the mirror and tried to focus on my puffy face. My eyes had already begun to sink in indicating the beginning of a major drunk. I shook my head, splashed water on my face and staggered back out to my barstool. What would be my fourth tumbler of Grey Goose vodka and ice was there waiting for me. Complete with olives. I chugged it down. Nice...real nice. The bartender leaned over and told me that that one was on him, but that Mr. Wick had cut me off.

"Bullshit." I said. "Here." I slipped him a twenty. "Pour me a double in a to go cup an I'm otta here." The young man pocketed the bill, laughed a little bit, and grabbed the bottle of Grey Goose and a plastic cup. Time to go home, I thought. I staggered out into the club parking lot and cranked the ignition of my Z3. I had left the top down knowing I would need to get some fresh air, but I didn't think there was enough air in all of North Carolina to clear my head. A bird had crapped on the fawn colored leather passenger side seat of my Beamer. "Shit!" I said as my head clunked down onto the car's black leather steering wheel. This model had a sport version fiberglass front end, which I bumped into the back wall of our garage when I finally did pull in to home. I knew I'd had a bit much, but I was thinking that I really felt OK. I gulped the last of the vodka in my to go cup, leaned back for a moment and sighed heavily. At least hitting the garage wall would signal the boys that I was home. If they cared. They had seen me hammered too many times before, so I wasn't worried about my appearance. I hoped the battle with Josh wouldn't be too dramatic. My plan was to ground him, send him to his room and go sleep the vodka, that was overloading my system, off. I just didn't need to have any more personal confrontations going on right now. It pissed me off that Josh had obviously been drinking before school for quite awhile and I didn't know a thing about it. I pushed out of the car and got into the kitchen without major incident. Eric my oldest son walked into the kitchen and saw me staring blankly at the pantry cupboard.

"Hey Dad. Looking for some dinner?" His deep blue eyes were scanning me with knowing precision. "Don't worry about me I already ate," he said. "I think Josh did too. He's upstairs sleeping." I started to say something, but couldn't get the words out clearly. Eric stared at me even harder. "Hey, are you ok?"

"I'm fine." I tried to mumble, but the words once again were incoherent. Eric really was a pretty good kid. He had recently turned seventeen. Probably the toughest of the adolescent years. Seventeen...the nexus of childhood and adulthood. Too much conflict. Too many choices. Too many chances to either do well or do poorly. And now that Mary was gone it was just that much tougher. Tough not only on him; tough on all of us. Maybe that was what was happening with Josh. Maybe it was just a reaction to Mary being gone. I was going to get to the bottom of this. But not tonight. So much for my planned father-son talk with Josh. I was still staring at the cupboards trying to put together some idea of a menu when it struck my vodka soaked brain that Eric just told me I didn't have to cook for them. They'd probably just ordered pizza. At least that's what it looked like when I focused on the dining room table. On it was a two-liter bottle of caffeine free coke and an empty Pizza Wagon box. I was glad I didn't have to think about a meal. My stomach flipped triggering a wave of queasiness. Eric looked at me with a queer stare and I began to realize why. I forgot he had just asked me if I was ok. No excuses but, after all I did have a belly full of vodka and no food down there to soak it up. "Yeah, yeah Eric, I'm ok. I just stopped at the club and had a drink in The Turtle. Are you awwright?"

"Oh yeah," he said. "I just have something to ask you and I don't know if this is the right time for it." I blinked twice, half burped, looked up at him and said, "No problem whasssup?"

"Dad, can you help me buy a car?"

My long day came raging down on me as the final problem, ironically the simplest one to solve, broke the camel's back. My short fuse hit gunpowder.

"Are you friggin' crazy?" I exploded. "You just turned seve—hiccup—teen. You got no job. You're no where nears responsible enough to take care of a car yet. So forget it. Period!" I didn't think I was yelling, but I probably was because my answer kicked off just the kind of battle with Eric that I was looking to avoid with Josh. Eric's face contorted to a confused, hurt kind of scowl. "This is why I didn't want to bring it up. You're drunk! I can smell you a mile away." He turned his back and began to walk out of the kitchen when for some unknown reason I grabbed a nearby glass and smashed it into the kitchen wall near the refrigerator. "Get your ass in here," I screamed. "Don't even think about walkin' out on me. I won't have it. I won't have it from your mother…not from your stinkin' drunk brother and I won't have it from you. Got it!" He turned, looked at me with more maturity then I thought possible and quietly, sternly said; "I want a car. I'm going to get one whether you help me or not. What's with you lately? My other friends' folks help them get cars. Some of them even bought 'em for 'em. Lately this place really sucks. I'm leaving." I wasn't looking at him anymore because I knew in my mind that I had done enough unnecessary damage and because I felt like I was going to heave. I knew I should have eaten something instead of drinking all that vodka before dinner.

Ten

Eric, by this time had realized the power struggle in the kitchen had shifted, he walked down the hallway and emphasized his current feelings by slamming his bedroom door hard enough to rattle most of the hanging objects in the house. I didn't think anything was falling, but the force of the slam rattled some fragile maple shelving, which hung on the wall next to his room. I was heading toward the bathroom to do my business and lunged forward just in time to catch a wobbling picture of him being held at the tender age of five by Mary, his mother. I stopped and stared at the picture for a moment and began to get swept up in the past. The two of them sitting on a gentle hillside in one of the pretty little parks outside of the small town of Pittsboro. We lived there when we first moved to North Carolina. Mary's green eyes and blonde hair. Her hair was beautiful, sweeping down in a gentle curve touching the top of Eric's young blonde head. Her pink sweatshirt; his blue one. Their eyes...hers dark green, his darkest blue...both so alike in so many ways. Tears had welled in my eyes when Josh popped around the corner from the bonus room and said, "Hey Pop, what's up?" It wasn't really a question. It was what had become a greeting for this faster than lightning generation made up of extreme games, turbo charged lifestyles and now, I find out, hard liquor. This was the generation of children that my age group, the vaunted baby boomers, had brought onto the Earth. Nice job. Before I could answer him, even though I wasn't expected to, Josh bounded down the stairs and was gone, out the front door. Wham! That was Josh. Always on the move. Never standing still. Apparently even with a hangover or a buzz still working. Josh had been a mover and shaker from the moment he spent his first night in a chrome steel crib in the newborn ward of St. Paul's Hospital back in Wausau, Wisconsin. God did that seem like a light year ago. I stumbled a bit in the hallway and thought of going after him, but I doubted that I could catch him. Besides I didn't have any idea of what I would do to him if I did catch him. Like most of my problems of late I decided to handle the situation later. Maybe Eric could clue me in on what was up with Josh's life, the drinking, the attitude, whatever else. I figured the boys would experiment a little bit, but drunk in school? It just didn't register. How could I have missed it? Once again the blinding obvious flew past my vision. The cold chill ran down my back again even though the house was rather warm. I thought I smelled perfume. Knew I had to be imagining it...or so I thought at the time. At least the little punk's quick escape had squelched my emotional trip down memory lane. I shoved my thoughts deep back into the special hidden pocket of my brain so rarely used nowadays and gently placed the picture of Eric and Mary back on the middle shelf from which it had almost fallen. Those shelves held so many memories of my life. Of our lives. On that fragile wood shelf, barely able to hold the precious memories that were entrusted to it, was us. The Wolters family. Past, present...no future. I looked at my Grandpa and Granny. Two wonderful people who were great examples. Grandpa the Granville Falls town physician. Granny, his devoted wife who was at one time quite a golfer. She even played with some of the greats in the early years of ladies professional golf. Babe Zaharias, Marlene Hagge, Polly Riley and Peggy Kirk Bell just to name a few. Granny was quite a personality in her day. It was so hard to envision what they were really like looking at this old black and white photo. A light haired man with his arm on a sofa holding his every present stethoscope and his young pretty wife sitting to the right of him on the sofa with her ankles crossed in the demure fashion of the day. So much promise. So much future. Those shelves held so few and yet so many ghosts of the Wolters family. Shades of what we were. Where we came from. Why couldn't they show what we would become? How would future generations look at photos of me? Of the boys? Of Mary? A wave of cold depression shrugged over me and I turned into the bathroom and threw up a third of a quart of good vodka. I left the bathroom and flopped onto my section of the queen-size bed in what was once the bedroom Mary and I shared.

Eleven

A restless doze left me thinking about why I never moved off of my half of the bed. I slept for a bit and then woke up starving. After eating some cold pizza alone in the kitchen I decided I needed a diversion. My stomach was cramping so I didn't think that I could finish a workout at the fitness center. That was my usual routine for purging alcohol from my system. I looked around the quiet house and found that Eric had joined Josh in getting out of the presence of their drunken old man. My depression deepened as I continued to search for something to do. I opted for working out in the garage. I had a small shop out there where I built golf clubs. I'd sobered up just enough to know that I wouldn't hurt myself with any of my club making tools. I wasn't sure what components I had in stock, but even if I didn't have anything new to do, or the right stuff, I was going to pull a few old shafts out of existing clubs and change a few of the "already been used" club heads anyway. I might even re-grip a set even if it didn't need it. And there was always beer in the refrigerator. That would help. That's where the peace of mind was hidden. Besides, I thought, a little hair of the dog might be just the ticket. It was warm out in the garage and I was glad that I had installed a medium sized Casablanca-style fan in the ceiling, which was just strong enough to push around the warm North Carolina early autumn air. I turned to a small black and white Sony TV I kept on a white wire shelf and flicked it on. The seven-inch picture tube was only large enough to reflect shadows of the images on the screen, but I never really watched what was on anyway. Usually I turned it on just to have some background noise while I worked on clubs. I started to work, and I rolled cold beer down into my growing belly. I scratched my gut which reminded me that I needed to up my workout sessions by ten minutes and add more ten push-ups and ten more sit-ups to the morning regimen. Sort of a ten for ten type program. At least that's what Grover would have called it back in the old days. Ahh...Grover...nope push those memories back down. Now is not the time. Just then my eye caught a shadowy image of what looked like a person swinging a golf club on the little Sony. I couldn't make out who it was because of the graininess of the picture, but it was too late for a golf tournament to be on TV. Besides, it was a weekday. The fan twirled above my head and I swore I smelt a familiar aroma that poked the recesses of my memory. Once again, kind of like flowery perfume...just like the whiff I had caught in the house. The sensation disappeared along with the picture on the screen. I chalked the whole thing up to the hangover. Back to the job at hand, I thought while I grabbed my heat gun. I eyeballed the racks of golf club shafts on the white garage wall and tried to decide what to do. "Maybe some woods." I muttered, but shifted my gaze to a row of shiny new True Temper Dynalite Gold iron shafts, which had been purchased for a prospective customer who had changed his mind. "Yeah, that's it." I said out loud, and moved to gingerly lift them down off of one of the top racks which held all of "Wolters Sticks Custom Clubmaking" inventory. Glancing up at the variety of lengths, colors, weights and styles of the other shafts made me realize that this once "little hobby" of mine had grown to quite an enterprise. True, I didn't generate enough income from "Wolters Sticks" to make a living off the business, but I had developed quite a reputation as a person who could build a quality piece of golf equipment. When I was sober at least. On top of that rarely did one of my clubs get returned, nor did any of my customers gripe about the price of their new golf equipment. The real delight though, came from being at the club and seeing someone using one of the sets I had made. Or better yet overhearing the club pro, Michael Tollefson, suggest to a member that he needed to go see Tom Wolters about having a "real" set of custom golf clubs made. "Done with care and affection, just for you." He would say in a mock Scottish brogue. "The best in the business Thomas "Moon" Wolters is. Don't let his looks fool you. He's older than he looks. And he's got a real feel for the sticks he does. Go see 'im. Make sure you do."

I began working on a new driver and thought, "That's me...Thomas "Moon" Wolters. One time husband of Mary, current father of two teenaged boys, top-notch businessman, single-digit handicap golfer, part-time club maker...full-time drunk. There I was getting on middle age. Getting a gentle paunch around the middle. Getting a bit crazy, and going to get hammered; again. I needed another Miller from the fridge. Twice in one day. "That's impressive," I said aloud with sarcasm. I set down a True Temper shaft and walked over the dusty concrete floor to the almond colored refrigerator that Mary and I had bought for our first home. I pulled out what would be just another of many cold beers that night. Thank God for the kind folks up at Miller. Thank God for the Plank Town Road Brewery. "God," I said, "how have I gotten to this point?" I stood in the warm, sticky garage in the North Carolina Piedmont and began my melancholy thoughts again. One son was out the door without a care in the world going who knows where, the other one had been upstairs wishing I would drop dead, and then he went off too. My wife Mary, with whom I had once, long ago made such great plans was gone...gone from me forever. My thoughts whirled like the fan above my head. The Sony blinked on again, seemingly all by itself. The shadowy image of a female twirling a club appeared along with a slight trace of a kind of rosewater smell.

Twelve

The LaFleur Mental Health Center was situated in a deeply wooded section of North Raleigh. A small clean pond decorated with a jet spray fountain placed directly in its center fronted the building. I noticed several pairs of people walking along a path, which traced the edge of the pond. Some paused to sit on benches situated near the path. Many were trudging around the water doing what we used to call the *"Mellaril Shuffle"*, back in my days as a nursing assistant in graduate school.

I hated coming here. I wouldn't be doing it either, but my damn family practitioner had butted in and had seen a massive depression blooming in my future. He demanded I get some help or he would inform the HR folks at QI. "Counseling," I muttered. "Counseling my ass. Just a bunch of poor misguided wretches with PhD's trying to tell other poor misguided wretches without such vaunted education what was wrong with their screwed up lives." I took my place on the concrete path of misery, but veered off to the main entrance rather than stay on the never-ending circuit populated by *the shufflers.* I had been in treatment with Dr. Margaeux La Fleur for nearly six months. I still had a healthy disregard for her brand of psychology and the promised success ratio the center and my busy body doctor touted. The entry foyer was littered with massive potted plants and overly cushy recliners. The patients in the waiting room made me queasy. I reconfirmed in my mind that I couldn't be as pathetic as they were. I just had a few minor problems to work out. Nothing big, just some normal crap. We all have problems. I just solve most of mine with Grey Goose.

"Hello Mr. Wolters," an overly friendly voice from behind a half-glass partition chimed. "Dr. LaFleur just came in. She'll be with you in a minute." Twenty minutes later I was sitting with relative calm in front of the good doctor, discussing my current situation at home.

"Tom, how was your relationship with your father?"

"Fine," I said. "Never really had any abnormal blow ups, just the normal kid stuff. One or two scrapes with the local police, but no real criminal activity."

"Who was your favorite relative?"

"That's easy. It was my Granny."

"Tell me about her."

"Well, she could have been the greatest professional golfer in her day, but she opted to raise a family instead. She married my Grandpa sometime in the twenties. She played with some of the great lady golfers kind of barnstorming around the Midwest doing exhibitions and stuff, but only for a couple of years. She really was devoted to my Grandpa and then when my dad and the rest of their kids came along she focused entirely on them. But she always was a great sports nut. We did all kinds of things together, football, croquet, softball, volleyball. We even played hockey on the Granville River during the winter." I paused and looked at the light gray ceiling. "She was the best at golf though."

"Why was she your favorite relative?"

I thought back for a moment. "I don't really know."

"Well Tom, when I asked you the question, you didn't even hesitate to blurt out that your favorite relative was your Granny. You must have some reason."

I couldn't figure out where she was going with this and snapped, "Who cares? What does this retrospective have to do with what's going on in my life now? Granny was part of my past life, my happy life. I need to get a handle on today." I felt myself starting to get hot. "Let's drop the ancient history and get me straightened out now," I barked at the good doctor. "I got shit to do!"

Dr. LaFleur remained frustratingly calm. "Tom do you remember one thing your Granny taught you that just sort of sticks in your head?"

"Yeah, she taught me lots of things...actually most everything. Particularly while we were out golfing." The past roared back into my consciousness like a rogue wave. "She used to lecture a lot. Some of it was about golf, but a lot of it pertained to growing up. You know...being a straight arrow...trusting in yourself...learning from your mistakes...the golden rule...fairness...honesty all that crap, but again I don't think this has anything to do with what's going on now." I drummed my fingers on the padded arm chair. "Let's move on!"

"Fine," Dr. LaFleur said. "Have you heard from Mary?"

"What the hell kind of question is that?" I glared at the good doctor. "No I haven't heard from Mary." I was beginning to seethe. "It's been four and a half months. Why should she contact me now?" I shifted in my chair and began scanning the walls of her office. Dr. LaFleur pressed on wanting more of an answer. "Well, I just thought since school has started up again she might feel like checking up on the boys, you know, see how they are doing." Dr. LaFleur cocked an eyebrow put a pencil in her mouth and waited. I contemplated getting up and walking out. Her office walls were neatly organized. Hunting scenery filled with ducks and deer stared down at me from the rich dark walls. I tried desperately to not look her in the face. The area behind her desk was a series of shelves stretching from one corner to the other. On it were several sections holding books by Rogers, Jung, Freud and other prominent shrinks. Dispersed between the wisdom of the psychological elite were knick-knacks of all kinds. Above the doctor to her right sat a statue of a chimpanzee sitting on a stack of books by Darwin holding a human skull in his hand, apparently in deep thought. To her left, and a bit lower, was a picture of her in not much of a bathing suit para-sailing in what looked to be some tropical spot; maybe the Bahamas. I wondered how they got that shot? Must have been a telephoto lens.

"Quit avoiding me Tom!" the doctor said with force. "Do you know anything about where she is? If she's coming back?"

"Yeah...yeah I know." I muttered as I sunk my head in my hands. "I hired a private investigator to run her down, and unfortunately he did." Thoughts of the first series of pictures and the accompanying report sent to me by Wilson McHugh, P.I. crashed back through my memory like a second rogue wave let loose in my sea of memories. Steamy shots of her and her new boy, clearly after a bout of tennis. His bare back facing the camera. Mary, in a too-short tennis outfit laying back underneath him. Hands entwined. Legs touching. The white bottoms of her outfit lying on the floor. It was too much. I began to crack, but quickly steeled myself. "Listen, you know as well as I do that Mary had too much time on her hands. When she quit working to take care of the boys it seemed like a good idea. But after the boys were in school full time and she didn't get right back to work...she, she just got bored."

"Tom, I'm not looking to rehash your wrecked marriage. I am just trying to quantify if there is any chance of a reconciliation." She put the pencil back in her mouth. "After all you are a successful businessman, fairly good looking, in the peak of your productive years. You are...whether you believe if or not...quite a catch." She smiled, but not in a seductive way. More like sympathy from an older sister. "And maybe, I just thought, that after a few months away from the nest Mary might wake up, realize how good she has had it and come back." Dr. LaFleur jotted a note to herself, put down her pencil and looked me straight in the eye. "That's all I wanted to know." The image of the second series of pictures, the ones with Mary, her boy and the two tennis pros, that came to me from Mr. McHugh complete with another written report flashed through my head and clarified my answer to the doctor. "No fuckin' way...it's over...period."

"Fine, done. Let's move on."

We spent the rest of my hour discussing the altercation I had with my boys, my plans to go to Wisconsin and what she wanted me to concentrate on prior to our next visit. She asked if I could bring in some photos of my grandparents and some of my mom and dad if I had them. I said sure and got up to walk out of her office as morose as I had been, maybe worse, than when I walked in. Prior to shutting the door I heard her say, "Tom, try to remember one thing for me ok?"

"What?" I asked.

"Remember who it was that whacked you aside the head when you needed it most. Because it seems like you need to get whacked again."

"Yeah, sure." I walked out thinking, "What the hell does that mean?"

Thirteen

The next several days went by without incident. It seemed that my success at work balanced out my failures at home. I made a relative kind of peace with the boys. First, by promising Eric that we would seriously go car hunting when I got back from my Wisconsin trip, but that I was going to have him pay for at least half of whatever kind of car he got by himself. Second, by sitting Josh down and lecturing him on the evils of alcohol. This talk probably did no good, but at least I felt that I made a positive first move. As he slouched out of the den, where we had the discussion, I looked at his back and wondered where in life was he going? Then I flipped open my daytimer and began to make final plans for my trip to Milwaukee.

Fourteen

The American Airlines MD-80 I had been sitting in cruised over Chicago and started it's smooth decent to Milwaukee's General Billy Mitchell Airfield. It had been a long two years since I had been back to the city of my birth. I knew that Scooter, the Greek and Duck would not have changed much, but I still wanted to see them. I had already, in my own mind at least, justified coming to Milwaukee a bit early just to see my old friends. Today was Thursday. Paul would meet me later on Saturday, for the customer meeting with the Thorvald Clinic people. The years I spent growing up in the suburb of

Granville Falls had been good ones. And in the current frame of mind that I was in, I knew it would be good to become just plain old "Moon" again even if it was only for a short time.

The Greek had given me the nickname Moon many years ago. As the MD-80 thundered on north along the coast of Lake Michigan and I thought back on what a strange route that not only my life, but my nickname had taken. Born Thomas Harding Wolters in 1954, I had spent the majority of my youth as "Tommy". Upon entering Granville Falls High School my buddies had dubbed me "Wolly". That name held until my junior year when I became "Wall Paper" after working as an intern for a decorator one summer. "Wall Paper" was shortened to "Paper" in college. Mostly because I was the only one in our dorm deft enough to handle rolling papers. I never advertised the fact, but it was actually my Grandpa, much to my Granny's dismay, who had taught me how to roll cigarettes using Bull Durham tobacco and some kind of cigarette papers held in a blue-green folder. Not long after graduation, in conjunction with the success of the Ryan/Tatum O'Neal film "Paper Moon" the label "Moon" was hung on me. It stuck. Moon I was and Moon I am, especially when back in Wisconsin. Each nickname carried with it a splash of memories, which seemed to crystallize themselves each and every time that I am called by one of them. The feelings all came back. The faces of friends. The ups of being in high school. The downs of being an adolescent. Warm thoughts of comfortable times once again pushed into my psyche, just like when I was back in my garage making golf clubs, and when I discussed my past with Dr. LaFleur. The mild depression which had me in it's grip was being held at bay, thanks to my prescription. By the time the wheels of the giant aircraft skidded along the cool tarmac of Mitchell Field I felt good. I was home.

Fifteen

After picking up a dog-ugly dove gray rental car from National, I headed north on I-94 towards Granville Falls. Once I got settled in my hotel I would call Scooter or maybe better yet just drop in at the bar. I knew that's where the gang would be. The drive to Granville Falls was an easy one consisting mostly of an easy skirt around the rapidly growing cluster of suburbs ringing Milwaukee then northwest into the prettiest town in the city's metropolitan area. My hometown. Granville Falls. The afternoon sky was a crisp blue, cut only by a few wispy clouds. Autumn in Wisconsin could leave you breathless. The leaves on many of the hardwoods were beginning to turn to magnificent shades of orange, red and yellow. I-94 had turned into Highway 41, which had become a four-lane road that curved gently up a series of small hills and then down into several low areas through which ran the Granville River. This was the familiar path that led to my home turf. On the right side of Highway 41 just after crossing the town line stood St. Joseph's Catholic Church. This beautiful old building was where Mary and I were married. It was also the home of the weddings of many of my closest friends. God, I thought to myself, the memories we created here in this quiet little place could fill a book. The church looked as holy as ever. Light brown bricks surrounded a massive set of double doors. A classic peaked roof culminated in a steeple that surely touched the hem of God's robe. Next door to St. Joe's stood the North Ridge

Country Club. This beautiful old country club was the site of another collection of great times. More great memories. My problems seemed to recede even farther away. Receptions, graduation parties, reunions, one too many funeral wakes. Looking back at old St. Joseph's I thought of the numerous times I had stood up as a groomsman for my buddies. Once I served as best man, for the closest of those friends, James Grovstrowski, nickname, for obvious reasons: Grover. I was deep in nostalgia-land. Four times I would walk down the long red carpet aisle of St. Joseph's in a different tuxedo. A few of the tuxes were bizarre 70's style designs of the day. One powder blue with a ruffled shirt and a huge crushed velvet black tie. One camel colored, with dark brown lapels and a matching stripe down the pants leg. Then there was my own. A classic black outfit with long tails in the back. A simple white bow tie and vest completed the look. Mary said I never looked better. I think she was right. No one in our group thought I could hold out and stay single, but I was fighting most of the girls off so far. If I ever did plan on getting married, which was not in my initial plan, I was determined to be the last. From all the gang that made up our high school clique I was the last to get engaged and I did make it in front of the priest who asked me if I was really ready to finally make the ultimate move. Many of the boys in the gang thought I would never find the perfect girl, first of all because I was intent on trying out quite a few of them. This attitude was extremely destructive and caused quite a bit of pain, but also because I was searching for perfection I thought I knew exactly what I was after. *The perfect girl.* When Mary finally came into my life everything changed. We were head over heals in love. She wasn't perfect, but she was pretty close. Lord knows I was far from perfect. Everyone in town knew that when we announced our wedding, the affair would lead to a match made in heaven. Preparations began in earnest. The pre-party, the wedding itself and the party afterward were slated to be historic. The entire community that was involved knew that this would be a good marriage. The big day came quicker than could have been imagined and I remembered my feelings on that day when, as I turned to look down the aisle of St. Joseph's, my eyes glistening, my shaking limb holding the arm of my new bride, I knew that everything would be magical. This was going to be the one with no end. A union of staggering proportions. A ceremony that all would remember. *The perfect wedding.* Unfortunately a few short hours later at the reception of the century, the first hairline cracks in our relationship appeared, and I was the guy holding the sixteen-pound sledgehammer that started them. The memories came flooding back as I pulled the gray rental into the church parking lot.

Sixteen

1980...Downstairs in the split-level apartment Grover, Scooter and I had rented shortly after finishing college, I heard my roommate crack open another Pabst Blue Ribbon shortie and call upstairs, "Moon, get your ass in gear! We got a wedding to go to!" I stood in front of a full-length mirror struggling with my eggshell white formal bow tie. "God-dammit Grover!" I said. "Get up here and help me with this monkey suit. I can't find my shirt buttons and my shoes need to be buffed. I'm a frickin' mess!" Grover was my best man, just as I had been his, and he had promised to make sure I got to the church on time, and in perfect condition. That was more of a task than he and Scooter had thought it would be when they promised Mary they could pull it off. Scooter walked down the upstairs hallway, which linked the upstairs bathroom and my bedroom with a pair of pink panties on his head. "Looks like Ms. Wilson left one last plea for reconsideration for you. I found these on the hook in the bathroom. Didn't you even let her get fully dressed before booting her out of here?" My head reeled as the events of the night before came back. "Shit no," I said. "Quit fuckin' around and help me!" How could I have let things get so out of hand last night during the bachelor party? Maybe a couple of weeks before the wedding, but not on the night before. I had to be at my best today and the thudding in my head began to pound anew. I scrambled back into the tiny second floor bathroom from my bedroom for some more ibuprofen and Zantac. “After last night are you gonna reconsider this move?” Grover smiled as he reached the top of the stairs. “Or you gonna do the right thing by Mar and stay loyal?” I shook my head and fumbled with the half vest, which was supposed to lay smooth over the front of my tuxedo shirt. “Who invented shirts without buttons anyway? These little silver jobs are impossible to get through the holes by yourself.” I opened the Zantac bottle after giving up on my shirt and vest, and dumped two peach colored tablets into my hand. I poured a small amount of water in a paper cup and pushed the pills down my gullet. The hope was that they would hold my jumping stomach at bay for the next few hours at least. “Grove! What the fuck are you doin'? Get up here and help me!” Grover laughed as he picked up the silver cuff links that would hold my shirtsleeves together and said, “I'm trying to figure out if you're gonna marry Mar, or if you're gonna fuck it up so I can have a chance with her. You know Cheri Wilson is hot on you." He pulled the panties off of Scooters head and said, "And after last night we got pictures to prove it." Grover leered a big grin at me. "Can you believe she did you in front of everyone here?" He laughed a squeaky kind of laugh and pulled Cheri's discarded panties down over his nose. "And she still smells as good as ever. WHEW!" Grover popped his eyes through the leg holes of the silky drawers and began giggling. Scooter and Grover were now totally out of control, so I threw a nearby towel at them and said, "Come on you assholes. This is my big day. We gotta get moving."

Seventeen

The three of us drove up to St. Joe's in a big black Lincoln Grover had rented for the weekend. The rest of the groomsmen were standing off to the left side of the church, by Father Frank's private entrance, drinking peppermint schnapps. "Where the hell you guys been?" shouted Mickey "the Duck" Mallard. "We been hammerin' here for a half hour!" The Duck's tuxedo shirt was already hanging out the back of his pants, and I noticed that he had just finished eating his boutonnière. I shook my head, grabbed the pint of clear, cool liquid and took a gulp. The rest of the service, and actually everything else at the church went off without a hitch. Nobody tripped walking up the aisle. Grover didn't forget the ring. Mary cried when I kissed her and everyone clapped when we floated down the aisle to the organ music booming out "The Wedding March". The pictures got taken, both the good ones and the goofy ones. We all hugged the in-laws, hugged each other, jumped into the limos and took off for the reception. Jingle's restaurant and ballroom was a huge barn of a place located two miles outside of Granville Falls near the north fork of the Granville River. Jingle's was run by an eighty year old German patriarch named Oscar Tetzlaff and his family. Tetzlaff had set up the establishment with a reception hall on one side and a restaurant on the other. The restaurant side of the place was famous for the traditional Midwestern Friday Night Fish Fry. A huge bar catered to the majority of the men's and women's softball and bowling teams in the area. Every night of the week, regardless of the time of year, either a softball game or bowling league was going on in Granville Falls so Jingle's and old man Tetzlaff had a pretty solid business working. With the addition of the reception hall, designed to be rented out for special events like weddings, graduations, retirement parties and such, the Tetzlaff gold mine continued to grow. So up to Jingle's pulled the caravan of black Lincolns and a train of wedding guests. The party began. Inside, Jingle's dark stained ballroom had been decorated like a Bavarian Wursthaus complete with oom-paah band and kegs of Pabst Blue Ribbon strategically positioned around the hall. The band members were dressed in lederhosen, but were capable of playing anything from Tommy Dorsey to Creedence Clearwater Revival. The request jar began filling up and after platters of sauerbraten, pork loin, roast beef and sausages were consumed with potato salads, fresh ground round, cabbage and kraut, the first polka began and the dance was on. By this time I had consumed at least two yards of beer which came to me in a special mug designed for just that type of volume and was surprised to see that Mary was hanging right in there with me. Each of our huge glass mugs had our names etched on the bottom part which resembled a fish bowl of beer. We had made a pact to limit the drinking to beer since we both had big plans for later that evening and hard liquor would put an end to the festivities too quickly. I had always been known to fall apart after a couple of tumblers of scotch on the rocks and didn't want that happening tonight. The band stopped for a break, and Grover was up at the microphone stumbling over his congratulation speech when he finally called for a toast. "Here's to swimmin' with bow legged women!" He stopped and shook his head laughing. "No that was at the bachelor party. I got a better one." He waited for silence. "Here's to the last of us...he married the best of us...God love you both...Tom and Mary Wolters!" The crowd cheered and I kissed Mary full on the lips. The toast was done and it was time for the bouquet and the garter. Mary tossed the bouquet high into the air as the band played "Pop Goes The Weasel". The unattached girls in the crowd had been circling the floor in anticipation of catching the bouquet and to the shock of all there...it landed right in Duck's hands. The crowd screamed at the reversal of fortune and true to form Duck promptly began chewing the roses out of the bouquet he had snagged from the air. While Duck smiled happily and munched away, one of the groomsmen blindfolded me with one of the bridesmaid's scarves. They had decided to let one of the girls catch the garter rather than the traditional "boys catch the garter" since The Duck had already set the stage for a reversal by snaring the bouquet. The boys twirled me around, placed me in front of Mary, and once there I began to run my hand up Mary's leg in search of her lacy white garter. The crowd roared and it didn't take me long to find it. As I wound it down her long smooth leg the band played their version of "The Stripper" which sent the guests into a deeper frenzy. The unattached girls, still not having gained a prize, swayed around me in a circle swinging their hips in a much more enticing manner than they had when they were seeking Mary's bouquet of flowers. I couldn't see them due to the blindfold, but from the howls of the crowd they must have put on quite a show. Having attained my lacy goal, I stood like a conquering hero and held the garter aloft. I turned my masked face upward and tossed the symbolic lingerie into the ballroom air. I pulled the scarf off of my face and watched in mute horror as it landed in Cheri Wilson's outstretched arms. Her fingers clasped the wispy item and as she locked her midnight eyes on mine, she twirled the garter in the air and touched the tip of her tongue to the top of her lip smiling darkly. I moved quickly back to Mary and proposed a toast of my own. I shouted at the top of my lungs, "To the greatest group of friends and relatives ever! God bless you all!" And we drank. I smiled at Mary and we drank once again, long and deep. I remember looking into Mary's dark green eyes thinking what a great day this was when Scooter and Duck began the chant of "Rat-shit". This was a rancid old drinking song from our college days. The pair, and then the rest of the gang, grabbed me from Mary's arms and paraded me around Jingle's dance floor on their shoulders belting out the raucous words to the song. At the end of the song, which my relations were happy to have end, we all were on the stage in front of the band. The boys hung me upside down over the edge and called for a reverse chug. Open went my mouth and down my throat, or actually up it, went twelve cold ounces of PBR. When they stood me back up straight the whoosh in my head almost put me under, but I called for a bathroom break and made a relatively graceful exit. In the Men's Room I stood over the urinal trying to focus. Oscar Tetzlaff always filled the urinals with ice cubes, trying to give the much used bathrooms an "elegant" look, and I entertained myself by trying to melt the entire bowl. I failed to melt them all, washed my hands and pushed the door to get back to the party. The door held fast and then opened quickly letting Cheri into the Men's Room. She shut the door as quickly as she had opened it and leaned back holding my only exit shut. Her hands dropped immediately to my crotch and began probing.

"Can you believe I caught your new little girls garter?" She said. Her left foot came up and kicked me back a bit towards one of the white porcelain sinks and I caught a full frontal view of her standing there smiling at me in front of the blockaded door. One of her eyebrows arched up as she asked, "What would you think of it on me?" Her fingers began to bunch the soft blue silk of her dress that moved slowly upward exposing her beautifully shaped young legs. Ankles, calves, knees, thighs...garter. I felt my resolve weakening as I said, "Come'on Cheri, let's go have a dance for old times sake. One more polka...or a slow one for you and me...I'm sure they can play *Hey Jude.*" She shook her head and said, "No way, we're staying right here." She smiled that crooked smile again, opened and shut her eyes quickly, visually grasped me a little bit tighter and said, "What are you worried about Moon? Everybody's outside whippin' it up. Nobody'll miss jus' you and me. At least for a few minutes." She continued to pull her dress up until I could see that she was wearing something that must have come from Fredrick's or Victoria's or somewhere equally exotic. There was barely enough material visible to cover what I started to want very badly. Cheri tucked her right foot behind my left knee and pulled me in close to her. I began to lose track of time, but by the clock outside our little boutique hanging over Oscar's bar registered twelve minutes since I had made my way in to the rest room. I didn't know it but Mary was outside beginning to get curious. "I wonder where Tom is?" She asked Duck who was busy begging her maid of honor, Holly Jacobson for a dance. Duck told me later that Holly looked up at Mary, over a foamy glass of beer, and said that she had seen me walking toward the men's room. To this day Duck still blames himself for what happened next.

Cheri was in full grasp of my situation as I leant back against the mirror over one of the men's room sinks next to a urinal full of ice. She held all that now morally and legally belonged to Mary in her mouth and I was not thinking of a single vow that I had pledged a mere six hours before. I can still hear the scream coming from Mary's mouth and the look on her face when she took in the situation and to this day I am eternally amazed that she ever took me back. But she did and from the end of the honeymoon night until the day I read the note letting me know that she had left...our relationship existed mostly in name only. For several years we put up a great front. Brought two children into the world. Tried like hell to convince everyone in Granville Falls and beyond that a one-time fling could not break up...the marriage of the century. But we were doomed.

Eighteen

Back in the present I pulled out of the St. Joseph's parking lot and continued to drive up Highway 41. I began crying. Tears came now and again these days in a spontaneous sort of manner. The shrink said this was ok, but it still pissed me off. Even though society said it was ok, that it was just our sensitive side, I still felt that men should not cry. Thoughts of Mary and the many counterfeit years of our marriage brought this bought of tears on. I had to shake the images or be mired in them for the duration of the trip. I wanted this to be a cleansing time. A time to remember the ups, not the downs. Lots of people didn't make it through their first marriage. Mary and I were just one of the crowd. "God...how fucked up is that?" I spoke out loud, "Marriage is supposed to work! Not get dumped in the trash!" The tears poured down. I needed to drive on.

Quicker than I would have imagined in my sight was the ivy-covered entrance to North Ridge Country Club. I pulled to a stop. More memories. My mind reeled again. I had caddied there as a young boy of twelve. And then later during my sixteenth year I waited on tables and served as a busboy in the grand dining room. Grover and I had first gone out to Northridge with the idea of getting jobs in the kitchen as dishwashers. A few months prior to me and Grover needing a job, the Duck had gotten work in the kitchen as a dishwasher. He told us to just go to the door, back by the kitchen entrance where the help came in, and talk to the cook. The cook might hire us on the spot, or send us to Mrs. McHenry. She was some kind of club manager or something. When we got to the club we walked up to the back door and smack into the chest of a man with the name Wo Fat stitched on his white cook's tunic. This two hundred fifty-pound oriental head chef, who ran the main kitchen of the North Ridge Country Club, scared the living shit out of us. "Whatyouwant!" he screamed. Grover and I jumped back and nearly fell out the door before we regained our posture.

Grover was never one to be shy and I heard my buddies' voice boom. "We want a job!" I couldn't believe Grover had yelled back at the massive Chinaman.

Grover had always been aggressive. He was a Big Rivers Conference champion wrestler. He was also the starting halfback on the Granville Falls football team. When he wasn't scoring touchdowns or running back punts and kickoffs he was chasing the cheerleaders. He wasn't that big, only five feet nine inches, one hundred forty pounds, but he was tough. And pretty good looking too. Along with the good looks and the athletic abilities was the fact that he had hit puberty in the middle of his twelfth year. Now at sixteen he had a beard like a twenty seven-year old Portuguese sailor, complete with long curly dark brown hair. The Chinaman was impressed. He barked a few more Chinese words at us and then in perfect English told us to go see Mrs. McHenry. Much later we found out that Wo Fat immediately liked the fact that these two punk kids would stand up to him. That was why he sent us to see Mrs. McHenry. We laughed in a spasmodic sense of fear mixed with courage as we walked to her office. Grover and I were figuring that since we got past the Chinaman we were certain to get jobs.

Back in the present I started to page back through the years. Mrs. McHenry, I thought to myself, as I continued to look at the North Ridge Country Club all this time later. What a lady. She was a flame haired, one hundred eighty pound, fifty-year old battleaxe who was charged with managing the country club. In reality her husband held the title of club manager. But as was also true in their marriage, Mrs. McHenry was in complete control. The memory continued.

Grover and I knocked on a large oak door. Many times that summer would this ritual lead to so many forbidden experiences. But this time was the most critical time for us. This was our first walk into the lair of Mrs. Allistair Dunhill McHenry.

"Come in" a voice chimed sweetly though the heavy door. We walked in and were nearly knocked down for the second time that day. This time not buy a huge hulking Chinese body, but by the overpowering aroma of the

Lady McHenry's potent perfume. I thought it was some sort of orange or rosewater scent, but very, very potent. There she sat behind an elegant French style table-desk. The desk had thin white sculpted legs which provided a strong contrast to those of the portly Mrs. McHenry. Above her head embroidered on cloth and framed in a perfect rectangle was the quote: "Someone has to take responsibility. I will!" -Sir Winston Churchill.

"What can I do for you boys?" she asked.

"We came to work in the kitchen!" Grover said with maybe a little too much authority. Anyway, I thought he said it a little too loud. I was wrong once again.

She took one look at him and said, "You are hired."

Her gaze shifted to me. Her large ruby lips curled and she cooed, "What about you sonny? Have you got a name?" She poked a strand of her deep red hair and purred, "What do you want to do?"

"Well, my name's Tom, and I-I want to work with him." I said pointing at Grover.

"I don't think so." Mrs. McHenry said. She gave a quick disgusted look at Grover and then turned back to me smiling. "You can report to Mabel. In the dining room. Have her fit you for one of the busboy uniforms. If you do well you may get a chance to make waiter!" She barked out a laugh and threw her head back accentuating her ample bosom. "Now out with the both of you. I have work to do." She turned to her intercom, pressed a red button and I heard her shout, "Mr. McHenry!! Get up here now! These ledgers are out of order again and you have some explaining to do!"

Nineteen

Grover and I walked down the heavily carpeted hallway of the North Ridge Country Club and tried to maintain our composure. We were shaking our heads attempting to figure how we had gotten so lucky back in Le Grande Dame's office. Just then we heard her massive door creaking open behind us. Mrs. McHenry peeked out and said to me, "Tommy…that was your name, right?" She waggled a stuffed index finger at me. "Come back in here. I need to see you for a moment."

"Yes ma'am" I said, as I slowly walked back through the large oak door.

"Sit down over there." She pointed to a chair by the bookcase. I'll be with you in a minute."

Mrs. McHenry finished speaking to her husband on the intercom, telling him to come up in an hour, and turned slowly towards me. The look on her face made me feel a bit squeamish, even though I was sixteen years old. I was confident that I could take care of myself in any situation, but I just wasn't quite comfy with this red haired old lady.

"Well Tom," she said. "Do you know why I chose you to work in the dining room rather than sweltering back in the kitchen with Wo Fat?" She once again rubbed a pudgy red nailed finger across her ruby lips. "It's because you are much too special to be stuck back there scrubbing the skin off of those soft white hands."

I squirmed as the hard cloth, which covered the chair I was told to sit in, worked into my back. Mrs. McHenry circled behind me and then moved to a closet in the rear of the office. She reached inside it and pulled out a bright red jacket with gold buttons down the front. A gold braid looped around the right shoulder. The jacket looked magnificent.

"Here stand up and try this on!" she snapped. "I'll do the fitting for you right here, right now, by myself." She slapped me hard on the back and forced me to stand straight. "I want all the boys in the dining room to be blonde and have cute little dimples just like you." She lightly pinched my cheek as she circled round me. "We keep all the dark hairy beasts, like your friend," she smirked, "in the kitchen with the other heathens." She circled me once again. "Boys like you deserve to be out front." Her circling continued. "Now stand up straight and stick your arms out."

I stood up even more sharply and pointed my arms out to my sides as Mrs. McHenry slipped the beautiful jacket on me. I began to feel like a sissy, but I had to admit that the jacket felt and looked very good. The inside was made of black silk. Dressed like this I felt like a million bucks and I knew that she thought it looked pretty good too. I could tell by her eyes. Mrs. McHenry spun me around and looked me over slowly. Her hands went lightly over the material. She puffed up the jacket at my shoulders, tugged at the rear to straighten the seam going down the back and told me to hold my arms straight up in the air.

"You are going to have to carry a large tray with dishes on it so you need plenty of room to move."

Slowly she showed me how to place my hands where an imaginary tray would be sitting, partly on my shoulder, supported by my left hand underneath, and with a deft grasp placed my right hand on a phantom edge of an invisible tray. Suddenly from behind, she reached around to my chest, straightened a fictitious bow tie and then slowly moved her fingers down the front of my jacket to button up the front of it. Her embrace drew me towards her a bit tighter than I thought it should, and my back abruptly stiffened as she slid her right hand down the front of my loose blue jeans. Her grip made me flinch.

"Stop right there," she whispered into my right ear. I felt the hairs on my neck pop up as she said, "You do prefer a woman, don't you?" Her breath was warm on my neck. The heavy scent on her was overpowering. "Even a more experienced woman like say me, to be fiddling about with you rather than the likes of old Wo Fat in the kitchen?" She paused and then said again, "Don't you?"

I began to lightly perspire, but breathed slowly and tried to fight off the fact that I did not particularly dislike what was happening. She continued, "Because I can tell you this my fine blonde boy, old Wo Fat will be in your hairy friends knickers quicker than you can spell Hang Chow once he begins working back there in the kitchen. You on the other hand will be safe...out front...with me." I couldn't see her face, but I knew she was smiling. "God only knows what Wo Fat would do to a healthy young piece like you." Her hands slid back out of my now bulging jeans and as she turned me around, straightened the jacket, patted my cheek once more, then she said, "Now get on out of here for today. Be back tomorrow at 11:00 am. Sharp! And be ready for some real work." She winked at me smiled and said, "Maybe we can play later on. Go on! Out!"

Twenty

My mind snapped back to the present, once again, as I thought about getting on into town. I continued to drive down Highway 41 towards Granville Falls when a curious inspiration struck me. It was much like that cold smooth shudder I had felt in my office while planning this trip. I recognized where I was. Immediately. This was exactly the spot where Grover had taken his Kawasaki 375 over the Runyon Creek Bridge. Fortunately for him he had died instantly. It was probably good for his young bride too, since Grover never would have been able to handle being in a wheelchair, or worse yet a quadriplegic confined to a hospital bed with tubes running in and out of every orifice. My thoughts of those early years and of my friend Grover tugged at an internal longing for the past, and how it had had an impact on me then and now with my current problems. Something was hiding here, maybe at North Ridge C.C. itself. Something that was calling. Tugging at me through my memories. I needed to act. Now was the time. I decided to go back to the country club and plow through some of those old memories. Maybe one of the answers to my depressed mood lay there. There in my past. I wheeled the rental car around at the next closest intersection and headed back to North Ridge. I was going to get a little better dose of the memories that had escaped me for so long. As I pulled through the ivy-covered gates of North Ridge Country Club I shuddered again. That curious little breeze was playing with my mind. "Right!?" I thought. I hoped it was my imagination anyway. The breeze continued to tug at me like a beacon in a foggy night. What was the source? My thoughts began to unsettle me. I muttered, "Where would these thoughts...these memories lead me? Nonsense"...I thought.

Twenty-one

The car rolled down the long, winding driveway that was lined with silver maples and the last of a stand of elms. Most of the majestic elm trees, which had peppered Wisconsin, were becoming extinct due to the victimization of the dreaded Dutch Elm Disease. The stunning drive, which led to the entrance of the North Ridge Country Club hadn't changed too much. Just a tweak here and there. The memories that had been swirling around in my head heightened to an even greater degree as the long two story main clubhouse came into view. The tightness in my stomach led to queasiness in my bowels. I reached into my briefcase for an Imodium caplet and swallowed it dry. The tension I felt turned to excitement as I eagerly looked forward to seeing the ballroom, the grill, the bar and even the kitchen again. I hoped they wouldn't keep me from entering the club. All I wanted to do was look around. Certainly no one that would have worked there back when I did would still be around, so I couldn't ask to see an old colleague or a familiar face. I decided that I would inquire about membership. Feign that I was potentially going to move to the Milwaukee area and had heard about North Ridge. "Is there a waiting list?" "Is this an exclusive club?" "Do you allow Blacks? Jews? Women?" I tried a few questions out loud to see if I could verbalize them without laughing. I couldn't. They were stupid questions anyway. After all this was the twenty first century. I would just ask about the price and about the waiting list, if there were one. There weren't too many cars in the parking lot this early in the afternoon, but the ones that were there were expensive. I looked at the names on the parking spaces as I walked to the entrance. Becker Paulson...Steven Wilshire...Mark Masters...Ms. McHenry! "No way!" I murmered. It would have been impossible for her to still be around. And what was with the Ms.? The old lady had always taken great pride in the fact that she controlled her weak willed husband by making even him call her MRS. McHenry.

As I pulled open the North Ridge Country Club's large front door, still a powerful oak, and walked through the beautiful foyer. That damnable slight stirring breeze crossed the back of my neck. It was warm. Almost comforting, yet a bit eerie. More of that slight odor, kind of like rosewater followed the breeze.

A voice called out from the dining room. "What are you doing here? What do you want? The club is closed today."

"Oh, I'm sorry," I said. "I didn't know. I was going to ask about membership here." The old woman with a bent back and brilliant white hair glanced up at me with suspicious eyes and murmured that it was ok, that no harm was done, and that I was welcome to come back when the club was open. I turned and started to leave the foyer as the slight breeze passed over me once again. Rosewater...why was that scent bothering me? Haunting me? On impulse I asked the old woman if it would be ok if I took a look around the club. I especially wanted to see the eighteenth green. I remembered that it was one of the most beautiful golf sights in the Midwest. The old lady said that that was ok with her, but that it would not be permissible to go out on the course.

“Thanks,” I said and walked out the back door of the club. Once back in the cool autumn Wisconsin air I was struck by a sight I had almost completely forgotten. The sun was just beginning to set and the fiery orange from its’ corona lit up the turning leaves in a cascade of brilliant fury. Contrasted by the remaining blue sky the scene staggered my senses. Though I thought I had my emotions in control, I was wholeheartedly swept up in the emotions of my past. The early years here with my folks. With my grandparents. People who were the greatest influences on my life. What would they say to me now? Would they be proud? Angry? Disappointed? If only they could counsel me now. I walked down the cobbled path to the back of the club. I turned past the caddy shack where my grandpa, my dad, myself and my brothers had all, at different times in our lives, spent many summers toting golf bags, learning to play sheepshead and telling adolescent stories each one a bit more wild then the next. The first tee box was nestled off to the left of where I stood. I turned right toward the historic eighteenth green and whistled a slow tune as I walked out on to it. The sun continued to settle in the west and as the slow darkness began to shroud the club I noticed a shimmering haziness fluttering around the eighteenth pin. The breeze picked up and again I was struck again with the fragrance of rosewater. I squinted through the lengthening shadows at the shimmer and tried to clarify exactly what it was. I couldn't. I was beginning to feel a bit uneasy. The cup on this final historic hole situated in the back right was in probably the most notorious position available on the eighteenths' modest expanse. I looked down the narrow gauntlet, which made up the eighteenth fairway and remembered the wonderful times I had spent with my dad and my grandfather walking up that narrow strip talking about the wonders of golf. But on the occasions when I played the game with my Granny Wolters was when I learned the true gravity of the game. How the game had evolved. Why people were so enchanted by it. She was a wonder. Elizabeth Mae Wolters had grown up in a modest dwelling on the south side of Milwaukee back during the early part of the twentieth century. My great-grandparents moved her and their four boys to Granville Falls just after the end of the war to end all wars. Elizabeth Mae had always been a big boned girl and a bit of a tomboy too. Her brothers forced her to play all the sports games with them since she was an excellent athlete and they needed her on their teams. Lizzie, as all the boys called her, was good in baseball because she could hit, ok in football because she was fast, but she truly excelled in hockey. The long cold winters in Wisconsin lent themselves to vigorous outdoor activities and all the kids with a pair of skates and hand-fashioned sticks took to the frozen rivers to play hockey. Lizzie was a whiz on the ice and because she was larger than most girls in the town, she could hold her own with most of the boy players. A few of the other girls in Granville Falls played hockey too, but mostly just as goalies. Lizzie was the only one of her gender who could take to the open ice. In her fifteenth year as her body continued to mature Lizzie developed a hard short slap shot that would carry her to greater heights than she would ever imagine. The wide icy expanse of gray blue frozen water would yield itself to wide green fairways pocked with sand bunkers and rolling berms all over the United States.

Twenty-two

The LPGA would not come into existence until 1950. But prior to it's inception many women excelled at the game of golf. But when the dreams of the original thirteen women golfers who initiated the group, all strong willed women, came true, the doors to the world of golf opened a bit wider for all women golfers. My Granny was a becoming a golf phenomenon a few years ahead of that gang of girl golf legends. The slap shot she perfected on the icy Granville River gave way to a hard, wrist driven golf swing. Lizzie Wolters found in golf a lifelong love. Lizzie became one of the first true travelling female golf wonders in the U.S. She wasn't really a hustler, because she would only play for modest amounts...she was more like a travelling exhibit. The things she could make a golf ball do were amazing, and people came from all over to either watch her swing or try to beat her on the course. Many would say that she was the greatest female player to ever come out of the upper Midwest. Some people claim she was the best male or female linkster to come out of Wisconsin. It didn't matter if she was recognized as the best or not. She pounded all takers on the course and walked off with their admiration as well as most of their money. She was tough. She knew the game. She knew how to win. And she was my Granny. Many people wanted to know why she didn't keep playing. That story was the legacy of my family. That story held a key to my current miserable situation. My Dad often times told me his favorite "Granny Golf" story. It was a day long remembered in Granville Falls that Granny Wolters made a name for herself. It was on that day that all our lives began to change. The time was back in the late forties when some of the men professionals were making their way to the Western Open outside of Chicago. An unlikely crew wound up playing North Ridge Country Club right in our own hometown of Granville Falls. These historic golfers were Ben Hogan, Sam Snead, Jimmy Demaret and Lloyd Mangrum. The foursome had ventured north to play our popular little hometown track, and to sample some of the fine Polish cuisine Milwaukee was famous for. Demaret had friends in the brewery business and promised the other three golfers that they would be in for a great time in Beer City. Snead had told the others that he had played a great little course outside of Milwaukee called North Ridge and that he would set up a match. It turned out that while the group was on the range warming up to play North Ridge on one sunny weekday, so was my granny, Lizzie. To this day I can still visualize her swing. It was smooth as butter. Back then many men teased women golfers, but they were common sites at most of the prominent courses. This day the foursome of pros apparently took lively notice of the young woman swinging away at a pile of balls. It was always difficult for me to imagine my grandmother being oggled at, but that's apparently what was happening. After teasing her a bit just to break the ice. Mangrum stood behind her and commented on what a great swing she had. Then he added in the disclaimer..."For a girl." Hogan, Snead and Demaret toppled over laughing when she topped the next three balls she swung at. My dad, who happened to be a ball shagger that day, personally experienced the exchange. This was why he could tell the story better than anyone else could. At the time he wondered about those three topped golf balls. He had never seen his mom do that before. As he relayed it, Granny took tremendous exception to her treatment by these men without regard as to who dished it out or how well they could play. She turned on the four pro golfers and said, "You boys think you are so good. Hah! I can whip any one of you four yokels nine times out of ten and twice on Sunday!" This made the four pros laugh even harder. Snead said to his partners, "Let's go get some refreshment and watch the little lady take the skin off a some of these here golf balls." He winked at her and said, "I think if she got the chance she would mean to whup us all." Hogan picked up his driver, stood over a teed up balata ball and said, "Well...if she can keep up with this...maybe she can." At that point the flawless motion that was Ben Hogan's swing began behind the ball he had previously put down on a glistening white tee. Back in a perfect arc the clubhead moved. Ben's trademark white golf cap never wavered, his eyes locked on the back of the ball as the club shaft hit parallel, paused, and began back down along the truest inside out path Lizzie had ever seen. She never saw the clubhead strike the ball, but the noise that came off the collision of persimmon and balata told her that she was out of her league when it came to the long game. It didn't even matter where the ball went. She knew that the others could at least match him for distance, if not accuracy. Undeterred she twirled a hickory shafted wedge in her hand smiled a bit herself and said, "Not bad...but do you have a short game?"

"What!" Hogan exclaimed. "Little girl, fun is fun, but I'm about to start getting a little bit pissed off at you." Hogan blushed and then added, "Pardon my foul language."

“I mean it,” Lizzie said with an appropriately demure smile. “I just know that I can keep up with you boys from a hundred fifty in.” She stepped up to a ball sitting on the level grass of the range, waggled her backside and clipped off a perfect one hundred yard wedge shot which landed right next to the pin on the one hundred yard practice green. She faced the four and with a smile said, “And I'm willing to put my money where my mouth is.”

Twenty minutes later, after much dickering and discussion, the four seasoned golf professionals and my Granny walked toward the first tee box at the North Ridge Country Club. My dad was carrying my Granny's bag. The pros worked up a decent side bet between themselves and then got some of the club regulars to tote their bags. It wasn't long before the group had a small contingent of very lucky local spectators tagging along to watch the show. Granny had proposed that the golfers all walk to the one hundred fifty yard marker on each of the holes and tee off from there. The par threes would be played from their regular red tee distance. When Granny described her rules for the par threes Snead threw up his hands and said that it just wasn't right for the men to take advantage of such a nice young lady like that. Granny told him to either put on a skirt or just shut his yap and get on over to the first tee box. Snead howled and said, "Miss Lizzie, I think I'm beginnin' to fall in love." So off they went. My dad was floating on air watching his mom lead Mangrum, Hogan, Snead and Demaret in a steady march past the tee box, down the fairway, on to a pair of little spruce trees which indicated the one fifty distance to the green.

"Ladies first." Mangrum said. "Make us squirm Lizzie." By now all the golfers were on a first name basis.

"Thank you Lloyd." Granny smiled at him. "I figured you were the gentleman in the bunch." Hogan noticably reddened and turned his back away from the spectators as he spat on the soft ground.

"No tees, just like we decided", Lizzie said as she tossed a gleaming white balata ball on the fairway. She began her pre-shot routine as she always had. Stand behind the ball. Focus on the pin. Breath deep. Stare at the ball and move to position. Light grip. Head cocked slightly to her right shoulder. Last thought: "Trust yourself." She pulled back low and slow. The arc of the seven iron she held in her hands was like a slow ocean wave swelling in the breeze on the way back over her head. The motion ended in a pause about three quarters of the way back then began again in the reverse direction. If the golf swing is executed correctly it looks effortless. Granny had told me many times when we were out playing to live life like you swing a golf club. If you move easily with poise and patience, life will give you back a great reward. If you slash and lunge at life it will rip and snag at you in a similar fashion. Her swing that day on that first hole delivered her one of many great rewards. The ball clicked off of the club's face, leapt up into the air, arced beautifully from right to left bounced on the front lip of the green and rolled gently to a stop six inches from the center cut pin.

"God Damn," said Demaret. "Looks like a kick in to me."

The men struck balls in alphabetical order rotating position after each hole. Granny was always first off. She later told me that she knew she would be in a position to win because the gentlemen would always let her tee off first. Her accuracy would put continuous pressure on them until the exact point when she needed to take advantage of her course knowledge the most. As I thought back on how my dad recounted the match I would always know that this was my Granny at her best. The ability to maximize her advantage when she needed it most was one of her greatest strengths. Demaret dropped his ball fifteen feet to the right of the pin and groaned, "I didn't know there was a hog's back in that green. Sammy, you gotta tell me this stuff. You been here before. I haven't. Snead snickered and said, "Sorry Jimmy, remember we got a little side bet going on top of our game with the young lady. You gotta fend for yerself!" The four male pros all had relatively easy par putts, but Granny walked off of the first green up one.

Twenty-three

The second hole at Northridge was a tough uphill par three. From the red tees it measured one hundred forty seven yards. This first par three featured a small plateau green surrounded on both sides by two towering elms. These elms flanked a six-foot hedge row at the rear of the green. A long narrow bunker protected the front of the tiny green. The only shot which would earn you less than par would be a towering fade. Because of the uphill grade only the top third of the flag could be seen from the tee box. Few golfers escaped with less than par, and bogey was a serious consideration.

"Whew!" proclaimed Hogan. "This here's a beauty. How many feet from the front of the green to the flag Lizzie?"

"Exactly twelve," she said. "No undulations. This hole is tough enough as it is."

Lizzie mimicked the routine which had won her the first hole but this time arced the ball from left to right, exactly the shot that was needed. The five golfers and numerous spectators watched as the path of the ball traced the soft Wisconsin sky and disappeared over the front edge of the green.

"That's gotta be close." Mangrum said. "Looks like we got our hands full boys. This little lady knows the ropes."

Lizzie smiled and said, "Step on up boys. Time to show me some of that pro golf shit!"

The pros looked stunned by this pretty young woman's use of profanity. My dad pretended not to hear. This time it was Hogan's turn to follow Lizzie. Her cussing must have been sticking in the back of his head during his swing because he cracked an uncharacteristic line drive that soared directly over the top of the flag. They couldn't see it land, but it had to be off the back of the green in the hedge row. The other three men hit mediocre shots which looked like they would pose no great threat to Lizzie's ball. When the group got to the green they saw that Lizzie's ball had landed a mere twenty-two inches from the cup. Hogan looked at her and said, "Now little girl, that's some golf shit!" He walked to where he thought his ball might be. My Granny tapped in as Hogan was still in the bushes looking for his tee shot. Snead, Demaret and Mangrum conceded the hole. "Two up after two," my dad shouted. "Way to go Mom!"

The men halved the next five holes with Lizzie. Their respect for her game was growing with each of her silky smooth swings and dead-eyed putts. Twice Snead asked if she could be bought out by offering her a steak dinner and tickets to the Western Open. Both times my Granny politely turned him down and asked him if he wanted the honors. Sam would bluster a bit and then smile before chiding her to keep right on with what she was doing. He reminded his partners that there was plenty of golf left to play. On hole number eight Lizzie stumbled a bit by pulling her tee shot into a tiny creek that ran down the left side of the fairly easy second front side par three. She hit a great shot out of the water, but Hogan had put his tee ball two feet from the cup and knocked the ball in for a winning birdie. The group halved the par four ninth and then stopped at the clubhouse for a drink. Lizzie...up one.

Twenty-four

My dad told me how he sat and stared at the group while he munched on a baloney sandwich and drank a cherry coke. He focused on every word the group was saying. The conversation went like this.

Snead: "Where'd you learn to swing like that Lizzie?"

Lizzie: "Well, I always was a pretty good athlete. Maybe it was the hockey that did it. Where'd your swing come from Sam?"

Snead: "It's natural."

Mangrum: "Natural my butt. Excuse me again ma'am. He never does anything but hit golf balls and fish. Hell, he hardly even stops to take a drink. But forget about him. Lizzie have you ever run across any of the big time ladies out on the golf circuit? You know I mean the Babe, or Marlene Hagge or Polly Riley?"

Lizzie: "I don't know Hagge, but I heard about Polly Riley and Babe Zaharias playing down in Texas during the '48 Open. At first I wasn't interested. I didn't really know who was in the running, but after hearing about those two going at it, well that was something. First Polly pounds on Babe in the Texas Open beating her 10 and 9 in the final. Then Babe comes back later on and whups Polly 3 and 2 in the Women's Western. I think rivalries like that...you know, the kind that you guys have on the men's tour could pave the way for a tour that the women could play in rather than just having occasional tournaments to play in. I'd love to play in a tour like that. I'm actually practicing so I can maybe qualify for some exhibitions or to fill in as an amateur. There are a lot of women players out here who could drum up enough interest to lay the groundwork for what could become a real ladies' tour.

Hogan: "Nice thought Lizzie, but it'll never happen. Not enough power in the women's game."

Mangrum: "I think it would be kind of neat to see the gals out there playing. With all that swingin' and swayin' there sure would be a bunch of men watching the action. You keep practicing Lizzie. Hell you're up on us four right now."

Demaret:"That's nuts. Remember we're not drivin'. There are only a couple of super talents out there like the Babe, Polly and maybe Peggy Kirk Bell. But that's about it. Not enough others to round out a field even though there are some bright spots like little Lizzie here. Come on. Let's go get the back nine in. The natives outside are getting restless. Word has gotten out that little Lizzie here has the four of us down by one with nine to go and I think half the town of Granville Falls has shown up to see what the world is going on."

Lizzie: "Jimmy...you call me 'little' Lizzie one more time and you'll be riding a putter!"

Snead: "God, I do love this woman!"

With that the group left the clubhouse and marched down the tenth hole to the dual spruce trees which marked the one fifty line on a wonderful downhill par four. This hole was not dissimilar in design to the tenth at Augusta. Lizzie was motioned by her four chaperones to strike away, and as she tossed her ball onto the downhill slope of the fairway. The sight of hundreds of fans from town made her heart race with excitement. My dad saw her taking in the moment and he whispered to her to kick 'em hard and don't let 'em get up. He told me later on that she giggled, calmed down and began what would become one of the most exciting back nines in the history of golf. Too bad so few people would ever hear about it.

Twenty-five

The first three holes on the backside were halved with ease. All five of the players had settled down into a comfortable routine. There were some very good shots from all, but none were truly masterful. The thirteenth hole on the backside of Northridge was normally played as a par five. It featured a two hundred yard carry off the tee followed by what had to be a lay up second shot so the player could pull off a hundred yard wedge shot over a wide round pond which edged up to the front of a severe sloping green. The trick was to carry the ball far enough back over the flagstick with enough backspin to hit the back of the green and have the ball spin forward to the pin gently enough to stop before it continued on down into the pond. The problem on this day was that the players were coming in from the one fifty markers. The standard one hundred yard third shot, normally hit high and soft would now have an additional fifty yards added on to it. The back to front slope of the green made this type of approach nearly impossible. Lizzie and Sam having played the hole before knew what they were in for. Ben, Jimmy and Lloyd thought they knew what was up, but all three were in for a surprise.

It was Snead's turn to hit first when the men would have their chance to match Lizzie's shot. Sam was thinking about what type of strategy to employ as Lizzie went through her patterned set-up. If she managed to keep the ball on the surface of the green he would let his partners in on the intricacies of the green. How it would have to be played so that at least one of the group could take the hole from this proficient lady golfer and go into the remaining five holes even. He thought that they would certainly be able to put her away on the back side with those kind of odds. If she were not able to hold the green, then he would keep this information to himself in order to gain advantage over his three playing partners since he was down to all three on their side bet. Snead hated losing in anything and prided himself on being able to seize the advantage right at the critical point in any situation, especially a golf match. This strategy, coupled with his extraordinary physical prowess and athleticism had won him many matches over the years. Lizzie pulled out what looked to be her standard seven iron. She pulled back low and slow once again and then unleashed a towering shot that began to the right of the green, arced ever so slightly in the air to the left, sailed over the pin and struck the ground a perfect two feet off the back of the green. Snead grimaced. He knew that the result of her swing, along with her knowledge of the green's undulation, would produce a shot that was destined to be ideal. His grimace turned to shock when the ball jumped off the ground and leapt an additional ten yards in the air and landed at the base of a thick oak tree. She would have no chance at a clean shot because the trunk of the tree restricted her backswing. "Holy Christ," said Snead. "Must have hit a rock or something." The four men sincerely expressed their condolences at what was just one of those nasty bad breaks that happen in the course of a round of golf. Lizzie was no longer smiling, but she didn't look shaken either. While Snead was readying to make his swing my Granny stepped over to my dad, bent down to his ear and said, "Cheer up there Billy boy. Remember once in a while you just have to take what life gives you." The tears that had welled up in my dad's eyes prevented him from seeing the competitive gleam that was flowing from Granny's face as she twirled her seven iron with slow deliberate rhythm. Snead landed his approach shot perfectly on the back of the green and his ball began to trickle down the slope of the putting surface. Just when it seemed that his ball had gained too much momentum and was destined for a watery grave, it came to a stop. Four feet below the pin sat his ball, leaving him what looked to be an easy uphill putt for a two. Demaret struck his shot poorly and hit the middle of the green resulting in the first of the group's balls to back up into the waiting pond. Hogan pulled his shot badly to the left and even though it remained dry, his chip would have to move across the sloping green and would be impossible to stop near the hole. Mangrum was a bit flustered by Snead being so close to the hole. He was up the most money in the men's side bet and wanted to stay in that position. He clubbed up one more than normal in order to make certain that he would fly the ball past the pin, but during his downswing he thought to lighten up his grip and compensate for using too much club and decelerated. His weak shot hit the front of the green and his ball joined Jimmy's in the watery grave at the entrance to the green. The crowd was chattering loudly as the five golfers strolled up to the very challenging green. Snead casually walked up to his ball marked it and moved to the side grinning and laughing with the local man who was carrying his bag. Lloyd and Jimmy, after desperately trying to hole their shots from the water's edge after accepting their due penalty strokes and missing, were chiding Ben to at least get close and make Sam work for his win. No one was even looking at Lizzie. She was standing with my father, over by the oak tree, looking at her golf ball. The crowd assumed she was cursing it vigorously. "I wish this damn tree would just fall down," said Billy. "Actually son, maybe we can use it to our advantage." She winked at him and said, "What you say we give it a go?" Hogan back in the left rough, struck a magnificent chip shot that skirted that high side of the hole but rolled off the front of the green and into the drink. Three of the five were out of the hole and Lizzie's chance at a decent shot was ridiculous. While Lizzie and my dad stared at the ball, Snead made a hasty putt that stopped just short of going in. He cursed the ball and tapped in for three. Unflustered by his weak attempt Sam called up to his final competitor. "Hey Lizzie, do you concede? That tree ain't gonna let you match my three!" My Granny placed her hand on top of my dad's head and called back, "No. No thanks Sam. Billy here just gave me an idea and I thought I'd give it a try." Whenever my dad retold this story he emphasized that he had not said a word about strategy to his mom, but he swelled with pride knowing that she would give him credit for suggesting something she knew deep in her heart she could do. She looked back at my dad, smiled and said, "Always remember Billy...just trust yourself. Even when you make a mistake. If you trust yourself with all your heart and learn from your mistakes you can turn those mistakes into something good...even if the mistake is just a bad break like this one here." She looked at the ball, then glanced up at the tree, then said, "Now give me my wedge and we'll put these boys away." The crowd moaned as my Granny grasped her wedge lightly in her hands, turned her back to the flagstick and appeared to ready herself to strike her golf ball directly into the big old oak tree. The four male pros looked at each other and shrugged just as Lizzie began her backswing. The wedge came down and lightly clipped the ball lifting it up with just a touch of the ground beneath being disturbed. The ball hit the oak with a lighter than expected thud, glanced high into the air and landed softly a few inches in front of the spot where it had first struck the ground and bounced at the back of the green. Now the ball began it's gentle trickle down the green and the moans from the crowd turned to a surging tide of screams, shouts and howls. The ball moved down toward the pond on a track that was written in the stars. Hogan, Demaret and Mangrum knew what was going to happen long before it actually did. My dad was jumping up and down screaming like he had won the lottery. Snead lifted his hat and scratched his balding head with disgust. And my Granny just turned away from the old oak tree and watched as her golf ball dove into the bottom of the cup on the thirteenth green for a two. The explosion from the crowd was deafening. The hundreds of people stormed the green and lifted Lizzie into the air. She bounced on their shoulders and waved her wedge high in the air. She was the golfer of the day and everyone knew it...even the men who represented four of the best golfers on the planet. The noise died down as Snead, Hogan, Demaret and Mangrum made their way through the crowd to shake Lizzie's hand. Hogan smiled and said, "That was fantastic." Mangrum and Demaret took turns kissing her hands and kneeling in front of her. Snead raised both his hands to quiet the crowd and said loudly so that all could hear, "Congratulations Lizzie! My friends and I concede the wager and the day." The crowd cheered loudly again. "You are clearly the champion and we humbly admit that you have whupped our butts." He joined Jimmy and Lloyd kneeling in front of her and bowed his head in sincere appreciation of her skills. My Granny had secured her place in the untold history of golf. Her legend grew as the story of how a young woman took on four of the best professional golfers on the men's circuit and brought them to their knees was circulated across Wisconsin from town to town. None of the pros ever disputed the tale even though it wasn't recorded in any list of accomplishments.

Twenty-six

After the match with the men Lizzie spent two short years touring with the likes of Babe Didrickson Zaharis, Peggy Kirk Bell and the rest of the early golf pioneers, but then quit the circuit. Many people began to ask about the pleasant young woman with steel in her gut and the golden short game. But Lizzie had settled back down in Granville Falls for good. On a few rare occasions my Grandpa would convince his devoted wife to perform again, mostly for charity events when the other lady pros came to the area. She continued raising my dad and my uncles and then in many ways us grandchildren, but in my mind, even though she was a golf legend, her most important accomplishment was that she became the greatest grandparent a child could ask for. She sat with me during the first Liston-Clay Heavyweight fight and howled at how the loudmouthed young upstart who chanted "I'm the greatest." took down one of boxing's legends. She sat with me and my brothers at Milwaukee County Stadium on Warren Spahn Day back in '65 cheering him on even though he was well into his forties. And then at an incredibly old age she sat with us in County Stadium again on Hank Aaron Day in '75 when the man who broke the other Babe's record came back from Atlanta to Milwaukee to play for the Brewers. But her greatest gift to me was the gift of golf. We would practice for hours at the North Ridge Country Club. She explained why the grip was so important. "It's the connection between your mind and the ball," she would say. She taught me how to look at a green and feel the break, decipher the grain and hear the beautiful trimmed bent grass speak to you. Golf was a microcosm of life's lessons to her and she gave those lessons to me throughout the twenty-two years of my life that she was around. If only she could help me now. I would ask if I could, "How can I play better? Not just golf Granny. Life. How can I play that better?" But most of all I would ask her once again to explain to me how the game affected our whole lives. My Granny was the best at knitting the experiences of life with the wonders of golf. Her own path had been guided by the game and she believed that the connection was vital. She would say, "Trust your experiences. Always trust yourself. Not only in golf, but also in life. If you hit it in the water on number three once, remember how, what, where, why and when you did it and don't do it again. Learn from your experiences! Use those mistakes to your advantage! If you do that, both in golf and in life, you will succeed every time. Or if you do fail again, you are well on your way to absolute success." Many times later in my life I had called upon those words and trusted my experiences to feed my thoughts and to guide my actions. Becoming an experiential problem solver was said by many of my supervisors at Manna, Thor and at GI to be my strongest leadership trait. Unfortunately of late I didn't seem to be winning life's decision making battle.

The shimmer that I had been staring at on the eighteenth green at North Ridge started to fade and as I blinked I thought that I heard my Granny's voice whisper in my ear, "Take life in your grip dear, don't let it grip you…trust yourself…you'll win." A voice continued.

"You are Tommy, aren't you?…Tommy Wolters?"

I turned quickly and was startled by the old woman from the club standing close to my side. She smelled of orange cologne. It was still overpowering.

"You grew up to be quite a dashing young man." She said. "I always did have good taste."

"You're...you're not Mrs. McHenry, are you?" I asked.

"Well of course I am," she said. "A bit heavier and the red locks have turned to white. But it is a beautiful shade of white. Isn't it? Say; let's not get maudlin already. What are you doing here? You haven't been home in years."

"Oh I have business up in Green Bay and thought I'd look up some old friends and stop by some memorable places. This is my first stop, but I sure didn't expect to see you still here."

"You mean you didn't think I'd still be alive and kickin'!" She gave a short harsh laugh.

"Well I am, they've tried to get rid of me several times but I have so much dirt on the pseudo-millionaires in this town they have to concede to my desire to stay on. They think they are so high and mighty running this club. But they're not so big! After Mr. McHenry died I didn't have much to do so here I sit. I'm like an old gold watch, tarnished and running a bit irregularly but still worth something. Come inside I'll make you a grilled cheese sandwich, just like the old days. We can talk about what's going on with you nowadays." She turned and smiled a smile that warmed me straight to my soul. "No hanky panky though! I'm much to old for that!"

Twenty-seven

After leaving Ms. McHenry I drove a memory filled fifteen miles through Granville Falls to where my hotel sat tucked in next to County Line Road. I checked in, hustled up to my modest room and hastily unpacked my overnight bag. I needed to I make an early departure to Whistling Straits on Saturday morning. That drive would take at least an hour. Things were really beginning to work out. It was nearly seven o'clock in the evening by now and I had promised the Greek that I would stop by his house bright and early the next morning. He said he had a great day lined up for us. I knew that I needed a good night's sleep to prepare, but I was hungry. I pulled out the yellow pages and looked through the *restaurants* section trying to remember a decent place to get something to eat. Years of living on the road had taught me that even though national chain restaurants provided a dependable meal at a decent price, the inevitable loneliness of eating alone becomes almost unbearable. A refuge from the storm, preferably a place with a local name, was what I needed. I always looked for and usually found that a quaint local restaurant with a good reputation was usually the best way to conquer the blues. I didn't recognize anything from the yellow pages, which was quite a bit larger than it was the last time I was in the Falls. I washed up a bit and then walked back down to the front desk. There, I asked a young girl sitting behind the check-in counter if the Lochmere Steakhouse was still open. She nodded and gave me directions. I asked her if it still had the best surf and turf dinner around. She said it was as good as ever and that she would be happy to call over and make a reservation for me if I wanted her to. Twenty minutes later I was sitting at the Lochmere Steakhouse's massive oak bar twirling an olive in my second vodka martini. I asked the bartender if it would be ok to eat at the bar. He said yes, of course and then proceeded to lay down a dinner cloth, utensils and more of their signature roasted cashews. "Another martini, sir?" He asked. I nodded quickly as I finished gulping the last of my second. He handed me a menu and began the preparations for my third drink. The clink of the ice he poured into the silver shaker made my mouth water. Even though I knew that I was going to order the surf and turf I was seriously gazing over the menu when I felt the presence of another person close by. "Not more of this rosewater shit," I thought as I turned around. The sight made me flinch and I felt my intestines strangle into a tight knot.

Twenty-eight

"Cheri! My God how are you?" I sputtered. Cheri Wilson, yes the same Cheri Wilson from *the wedding.* Long before our scene in Tetzlaff's men's room Cheri had been the first girl I ever danced with. That seemed like a million years ago. Our first embrace took place at the James Madison Middle School seventh grade holiday dance. Even to this day I remember how she smelled. I am certain the fragrance was *Love's Baby Soft.* I could actually feel the motion of the two of us swaying back and forth on the packed gym floor. Cheri was dressed in a slightly stiff pink mini-dress which was delicately being crushed against my gangly young body to the strains of *"Let It Be"*. That Beatles classic was followed close behind by another... *"Hey Jude"*. I didn't let go of her and we just kept dancing on through the rest of middle school. I couldn't quite remember why, but we broke up shortly after high school began. "Tom! I thought that was you." God, still a great smile, I thought. She hugged me tight as she continued. "But I couldn't imagine how it could be. I thought you lived down south, in North Carolina or somewhere. You look great. What have you been up to?" She still had the mildly irritating habit of firing off questions at breakneck speed in a voice that made my elbows quiver. I was amazed that she could still have this type of effect on me.

"I'm up here on a business trip and thought I'd come in a day or so early and spend some time with Greek, Duck, Scooter and the boys." I was really shook up but blurted out.

"I'm surprised to see you." I then tried to regain some control over my emotions by being boring. "What's been happening in your last twenty years?" She smiled at me and said, "Oh the usual. Good job. Lousy husband. Gorgeous kids. Ugly divorce. You know the story. Lonely middle-aged lady sitting at the local gin mill waiting for a drink when..." She waved for the bartender to come over as she continued to talk, "...BOOM, lo and behold she runs into a long lost love." Her head tilted. Her familiar crooked smile beamed. Her dark hair swung around her shoulders. I began to lose it again. "Just the usual," she finished. I smiled back at her and demanded that she join me at a table for dinner. I told her that I was going to buy her the best meal in the house and she owed me an update that was long overdue. We moved to a corner table, shared a Midwest style surf and turf and ordered after dinner drinks. Even though I was beginning to get loaded I was able to hold up my end of the "trip down memory lane" conversation. The evening progressed at a fast pace. This was really better than I could have imagined especially since the last time I saw her was in the men's room at Oscar's. My memories of Cheri from middle school began to blur with the real woman who was sitting across the table from me at the moment. More than once during our memory trip to the past her leg brushed against my ankle. I wrote it off as a fluke at first, but it kept happening. Finally, just as I was beginning to not be startled by the occasional touch, her now shoeless foot crept up the bottom of my left trouser leg. My insides seized again as I took a good look at her. Cheri had held on to her figure. It was wonderful for a woman in her mid-forties. She still stood about five feet tall, the same as her height was in high school. Her hair was still black as night. I couldn't detect any hints of coloring but it wouldn't have mattered if I had. She looked extremely attractive to me and the first thoughts of a tryst began to formulate when our second order for stingers went to the bartender. She gabbed easily about our past, conveniently not bringing up the wedding incident. We laughed about the times we went ice skating together. I blushed when she talked about the first time I kissed her in the old Falls Theater. She frowned when she reminded me of how cold I acted when I broke up with her after the Homecoming Dance our Freshman year. She said that it hurt very much, deep inside her. She was confused as to why we rarely spoke to each other after that night. She began dating older boys. Many were going to school at Marquette University. She went on to school there, following one of her beaus, and graduated with honors in business administration. I went on to the University of Wisconsin in

Madison and lost track of her until our little performance at the wedding and the night preceding it. Then she said something that struck me right in the chest. “I never did know why you dumped me back in High School, and then a second time prior to getting engaged to Mary. That move seriously confused me.” She began to smile in a nasty sort of way. “Care to explain?”

I gulped down the last of my current stinger and tried to focus on her dark moss-green eyes. She smiled almost crookedly and tilted her chin downward just a bit.

“Well?”

“Look Cheri” I said, “it was light years ago. Who knows what was going through my head back then? You know most boys at that age have their brains in the wrong head, and then the wedding thing, well you know.”

I was unbelievably uncomfortable now even though she was stroking my leg with her foot in a slow constant rhythm. “Well Tom,” she said. “It wasn’t like we were all that close back in high school. Middle School was fun but we lost it in High School. Prior to you running off and getting married I wanted to see what I was missing.” I ran my hand through my hair and said, “Yeah but Cheri, on my wedding day? That was more of a full frontal attack. I wasn’t quite prepared...you know?” Her mouth turned down in a mock pout. “Does that mean that you would not have broken up with me if we would have gone farther in high school down in your recreation room?”

“No, No, No,” I said. “We always had a good time. You were great.”

“But I wouldn’t go all the way. Was that it?” she asked. Just after those words came out she quickly touched the tip of her tongue to her lips and hummed. “Well we went all the way prior to your going and getting married and it still didn’t get us together. What about that?” My eyes blurred a bit and I realized I was a little more than just tipsy. "I dunno. I always was a little dense when it came to you. Maybe I was intimidated back then." She grabbed at the opening. "Well are you intimidated right now? 'Cause if your not I've got a couple of pretty good ideas working." She smiled so broadly that I could see almost every one of her perfect white teeth. I smiled back and said, "Well, better late than never I guess." Her toes curled around the top of my left sock and began to tug in a very gentle way. She dipped her finger into the chunky glass holding her stinger, slipped her pinky between her slightly open lips and said, "Let's go."

Twenty-nine

The next morning hit home with that all too familiar fuzz of pain and pleasure. I still had a lot of whatever we were drinking in me and the uncomfortable knowledge that we had done some illegal things too. My nose burned and the back of my throat was raw. I came to full consciousness when I heard: "Mom, I have to get to work! Get up! I'll be out in the car!" One blurry eye focused on the back end of a short plaid skirt storming out of the bedroom I was in and a flash thought of Egg Jiffies from the Jiffy fast food chain struck me. Egg Jiffies were wrapped in the traditional plaid of the nationwide fast-food chain. The minimum wage employees were wrapped in plaid too. I guessed that Cheri's daughter was employed as one of the Jiffy Girls. Even through my blurry eyes she looked pretty cute from the back end. Just like her mother. I gagged and coughed when I rolled my numb head to the right and stuck my face into Cheri's stubbly armpit. Shit! I almost puked. I had done it again. Sure I was out of town. Yeah, Eric and Josh would never know. I had no real obligation to Mary. But now I had to face Cheri. And no matter what has been read, filmed or discussed about "found lost love" it just isn't true. Particularly when you are in the psychological state that I was currently in. The situation was made worse by the fact that Cheri rolled toward me, kissed me on the ear and whispered, "I always did love you."

"God Cheri, I hope we didn't embarrass your daughter."

"Don't worry about it." She said. "She's a big girl. Hey I have to get her to work. Can we meet for lunch? How about at the Dutchland Dairy? It'll almost be like one of our first dates." Back to the non-stop talking. "I have a few things to clear up at my office, but I can be there by 11:30 that way we can beat the rush. You're welcome to sleep in here 'til then, ok?" "Yeah, that sounds great," I lied. "See you around 11:30." I turned back to my warm spot as I felt her slide out of bed and head for what must have been the bathroom. I peeked at her naked figure walking away from me. No matter how nasty I felt, my male desire kicked in again and I followed her into the steamy shower. She did have a great body. After we were done, Cheri jumped out dried and dressed quickly as I crawled back into her bed. An hour later I woke up and felt pretty good. Hungry though. In the kitchen I toasted some bread, made some instant coffee and thought about what I should do. I glanced around the Wilson's kitchen and wondered what I had said the night before. What would she expect? I didn't remember her talking about any children. I wondered if there were others. I walked through the entire house and found it uninhabited. Next I took a quick shower and did the honorable thing. I bolted.

Thirty

As I drove down Appleton Avenue I knew that I would never see Cheri again. And that thought did not depress me even though I still had a pleasant feeling in my loins. She did look good walking into the bathroom. And that quickie in the shower was damn near perfect. God I felt like a shit. Another cut and run session with a woman I once was serious about. What a hero. I shook off the short lived tryst and thought about the day ahead of me. It was time to go meet the Greek and Duck. On the drive out around Granville Falls I passed nearby the cemetery which held our family plot. My thoughts turned again to my Granny and Grandpa. What the hell. A little detour wouldn't hurt. Greek and Duck could hold on. I decided to drive up and sit by the headstones for a few minutes. My hangover was now beginning to kick in in gale force. A Diet Coke and some fresh air would help push it back for a few hours. Maybe a big bag of Cheetos would quell the sour feeling in my stomach. A half-mile down from the cemetery was a Kwikie Trip gas station. I knew I could get the necessary hangover remedy ingredients there, so I turned in and bought the groceries. I headed up to the cemetary to find the family plot and after searching around a bit I found our markers. Two hours later I woke up in the cemetary. I was lying on my back on some very hard ground. My back was killing me. I knew I had to get over to the Greek's house, but something was pulling me or holding me to this spot. I still couldn't see too well due to my bloodshot eyes and fuzzy brain, but I thought I could smell rosewater again. I rolled to my left and gasped. My Granny was standing next to a tree holding a hickory-shafted putter. The look on her face was one of mild disgust tinged with anger. It looked like she wanted to plant the putter between my eyes. A wild thought hit me that it might actually relieve the pain in my forehead.

"You're a real sight," she said. "I've been watching you since you rolled into town. Get up! We need to talk."

I tried to move my mouth but the sounds coming out were just muffled blubs. "You...you're...you're dead," I whispered. "You're dead."

"Yes I am." She snorted. "So what? You look ridiculous."

Her reply was so matter of fact that I missed the true meaning of her words. The putter swung slowly in her hand like a pendulum moving through thick water.

"As a matter of fact," she said, "you look kind of dead yourself." Her figure moved around me in a slow circle. "Pretty impressive. If you weren't my favorite grandchild I would have left you to gag on your own vomit." I reddened. She continued, "You don't have to tell me how you got this way. I've been watching you for a long, long time. You've been having quite a time of it. How you went and screwed up your marriage kind of hurt me, but you sure did raise some good looking kids. At the moment it's hard to believe they come from your stock." Granny began to walk a bit faster and she twirled the ancient putter quicker as she gazed down at me. I tried to sit up and couldn't quite get it right.

"Don't try to move just yet," she said. "I'm holding you down there until I make a point or two." The putter head stopped directly in front of my face. "I don't have much time so listen up good. This isn't you. You aren't a wasted up drunk with no confidence. Here's a hint for you. Don't try to plunge back trying to fix everything that went wrong. You can't." She moved her putter over her shoulder and told me to look past an old oak tree that was standing a short ways off. At once I was able to maneuver enough so that I could see what she was pointing at. It was my buddy Grover's headstone. "Last time you were here that oak over by Grover's plot was a might shorter," she said. I pulled myself up and put my hand on Grandpa's headstone then I laid my other hand on Granny's. I had forgotten that that was where I decided to take my nap. I felt another ghostly surge and looked three rows of stones to the left at Grover's grave. His image was hazier than Granny's was, but I knew it was him. I tried to see him better, but thoughts of some kind kept pounding in my brain. I thought they were coming from him, but I wasn't able to make them out.

"You should touch your roots more often you know."

What looked like Granny's hand lay on my shoulder as she continued, "I always told you to just trust yourself. Play life like you play a course. Be confident that you'll make the shot and if you don't, if you screw up then learn from it. Use your mistakes to make you better. Not worse. Not worse. Not worse..." Granny's image began to fade.

My head slammed down on to the corner of her red granite headstone. I looked up and she was gone. So was the image of Grover. I shook my head. Did that really happen? I wondered if it really had, or if I was suffering from the hang over of the century. Maybe some of the junk Cheri got me to try was laced with some bad shit. Granny couldn't have really been there. "No way!"

Thirty-one

I rang the doorbell of the mid-sized brick colonial where The Greek lived. Before the door opened up I glanced up and down Robin Hood Lane. middle class suburbia was written everywhere. All the mailboxes looked the same. Most of the houses looked the same. Even the dogs in the yards looked like they came from one litter. Numerous minivans lined the perfect paved driveways like a soccer mom parade. Marcia, the Greek's wife, opened her front door and shrieked my name. "Moon!"

We plunged through the house, grabbed a cooler of beer and crashed onto the patio laughing and talking non-stop all the way. I always liked Marcia. I even had a crush on her back in the day. Nothing ever came of it, although I did hit it off with some of her best friends. It was because of our non-entanglement that we had stayed so close over the years. Finally when our personal reminiscence was over I broke the ice with a question I half dreaded to ask.

"How's the Greek?" I asked.

"Oh," she stopped smiling. "He's ok. Now that he's working again. But it was touch and go for awhile." Her forced smile turned sad. "I couldn't get him to do anything after the accident. He was drunk or stoned all the time. What really broke my heart was that the kids started to make fun of him. Then he really plunged. He started to hang around with the sleaziest group of deadbeats you ever saw. Even Duck and Willie couldn't bring him around."

"Why didn't you call me?" I said, "I would have been up here in a flash."

Marcia smiled with small tears in her eyes. "I know, but your life was moving on. North Carolina is a long ways away. We all keep hearing about your success." Her brilliant smile came back. "Are you a millionaire yet?" She held up her hands. "No! Don't tell me. I couldn't bear it. Anyway I know the Greek couldn't. God he still worships the ground you walk on." She looked away fighting back tears. "Listen enough of this. You have to go see him. He'll be at Scooters by now. Maybe some of the rest of the gang will be too." I stood up and asked, "What about you?" "Go on by the time you get home I'll have dinner all ready and we can keep talking old times and then start on today forward. You still haven't told me shit about what you're doing now." God, she was damn near perfect. I hugged her close and whispered, "God Marcia, I miss you." I squeezed her hard and said, "Thanks." Then I pulled away and drove off to the hallowed ground where so much of my mis-spent youth occurred...*Scooter's.*

Thirty-two

The Greek, Duck and Scooter were huddled over the curved end of Scooter's long pine bar. Beer coasters from around the world were inlaid all along the lacquer-covered bar. The brass rail near the stained floor had held up many tired feet since I had last place mine on it. The SmokeEater on the far wall above the filthy Pabst Blue Ribbon clock cranked away in a never-ending effort to clear unclearable air.

"Moon!!!"

All three of my buddies turned and howled my name at the same time.

"Set 'em up!" yelled the Greek. "Moon's home!" Scooter plunged his hands into the old ice filled beer chest and pulled out four frosty bottles of Miller Genuine Draft. Without breaking his motion four jiggers of brandy were poured out and topped off with a touch of peppermint schnapps in each.

"Here's to you Moonie! Good to have you back in town. Whatcha been up to and what the hell are you doin' here?"

"You know I can't stand being away from you guys for too long. No matter what you think." I shouted at the Greek as I threw down the jigger and gulped half my glass of beer. "Hey Greek, Marcia looks great. I just stopped over at the house and popped her for old time's sake." I pulled my face in a mock gesture and kissed the air. "You're off the hook for at least a few weeks. Course now she'll be moaning my name every time you get on top." I winked, "If she ever wants you back that is!"

"You asshole!" Greek laughed. "You couldn't make her happy with help from Mel Gibson. Come on its time for another Abber Gut."

Three hours later the four of us were a stumbling, laughing pile of juvenile coyotes. Two full quarts of brandy and nearly a fifth of schnapps were history. God only knows how many beers we had thrown down and how many old stories we retold. We were a mess.

"How the hell are we going to get home?" I asked.

"Gimme the phone Scooter...I'll call Marcia." Greeks words tumbled out of his mouth in a series of spits, slurs and grunts, but we all knew exactly what he meant. Scooter dialed the phone and began pouring what was termed by our gang..."the last mile". The history went like this.

Years before when we knew we were all toasted at least too toasted to drive, we devised the last mile to ensure that no one would go the way of Grover. As crazy as we all were one funeral for a friend was enough. We were camped out at Snapper's Keg one night, pickled out of our gourds, and started to talk about someone who was capable of sobering up. Scooter, who always had wanted to run a bar, blurted out that he knew a sure-fire method of sobering up. Or at least a way of straightening out our heads for long enough to drive about ten miles. He told me to lay down on the bar and hang my head over the edge. I was too shitfaced to argue so up on the bar I went. He said, "Open your mouth and try this. If it works you drive tonight and then you won't have to drive again 'til we all make it through the circuit. The circuit, being each one of the four of us. That way you'll only have to go the last mile once every three times we go out. Four, five or six if we got more guys with us."

"Ok," I said. I'm game."

So back went my head and into my mouth went a raw egg, a shot of extra sharp ginger brandy and a full jigger of Tabasco sauce. I immediately puked a liquid fire bolt of fluid that had made it's way down to my stomach before rebounding at the bottom and spouting out my mouth and out both of my nostrils. I felt like someone jabbed me with a hot poker, but my head was clear. I had sobered up. We got home safe. And the last mile was born.

"You ain't been around for awhile Moon," said Duck, "so you gotta do the mile. Just for old times sake!"

At any other time that may have scared the drunk out of me, but not tonight. Besides I figured I didn't really have to drive since I knew Marcia would be coming to pick us all up. As I positioned myself on the bar all I could think about was what they would say back at QI if they could see me now. Then the crowd began to chant..."Moon, Moon,

Moon...MOON!" The cheers became roars. I closed my eyes and actually enjoyed feeling the hot gooey liquid roar down my throat. I waited for the inevitable reverse peristalsis...but it never came. I gulped hard once. Sat up. Then howled for another beer. Scooters exploded. The clientele screamed for a free round. The taps began to flow and the last thing I remembered before my face hit the floor was pulling out a hundred dollar bill and slapping it into Scooters pocket saying, "Thakks bubby!" Then boom! Down I went like a ton of wet cement.

Cold tile on a hung over face feels good. Real good. My stomach on the other hand felt bad. Real bad. That thought registered in my soaked brain just as the rumble in my gut hit a peak. I got my head over the bowl just in the nick of time.

"Thank God you hit the bowl this time." Marcia sighed. "I'm sick of cleaning up your puke. You were supposed to help me with the Greek not turn into him." She clicked her tongue and said, "After you left, I thought about it and I knew I should've gone with you to Scooters." Then she turned away from me and walked down the narrow hallway mumbling something about a friggin' idiot. I guessed that that was me.

I pulled away from the Greek's house knowing that I'd let Marcia down but that I had re-cemented friendships that would never die. As I drove down Main Street on the way out of town I was thinking to myself how odd it was that I could still feel pretty good about getting hammered with the old gang, and that I was ok regarding my brief tryst with Cheri, but that the encounter with what I thought might have been my Granny and Grover or their ghosts just could not have been real. Alcohol, lack of sleep and whatever Cheri had slipped me must have rattled my brain. I did not believe in ghosts. I never have believed in them. And I was not going to start now. As I left town driving North, the sun shone bright on the multi-colored oak leaves of the ancient trees running down Main Street. My nostalgia trip back to Granville Falls had been a mild disaster. I squinted my eyes into the rising sun, sighed deeply and chose to move on down the road. I had to meet Paul in Kohler. Whistling Straights and Black Wolf Run were waiting.

Thirty-three

Just over an hour later, heading due North on I-43, I rendezvoused with Paul just off of the Sheboygan turn-off; Exit 126, Wisconsin State Highway 23. Old Hwy 23 led straight into one of Wisconsin's most beautiful little towns...Sheboygan. I pulled my rented road heap off the side of the pock marked, pot hole strewn road. Paul had been waiting for over an hour and when he saw me he said, "What the fuck happened to you? You look like shit!" I briefly explained that I ran into some old buddies down in the Falls, and kept the details to a minimum. Paul looked at me with a skeptical eye and probably figured it wouldn't do any good to start lecturing me at this stage of the game. "For Chrissake Tom. We got business to do today." Paul shook his head and continued, "Well, try to pull yourself together. All we really need to do today is play golf. You should be okay to entertain by dinnertime." We rolled west down Wisconsin Highway 23 towards Kohler and decided to check in at the American Club before we headed up to the town of Haven. Haven was the last tiny bit of civilization one could hit prior to rolling through the big stone gates of Whistling Straights, site of the 2004 PGA Championship. We could hardly wait to get there, but it made more sense to check into the hotel first. Upon turning south on County Trunk Y signs for the American Club began to pop up. The road was neatly lined with trees, both young and old. They looked like wooded sentinels guarding this wonderful rural setting. Smokestacks from the old Kohler Co. plant could be seen to our left, which meant that the now famous American Club was coming up on the right. As we drove along, County Trunk Y had become Highland Drive. We drove past the Kohler Design Center, the Kohler Waters Spa and headed down a beautiful drive. This nearly straight pavement led to the Carriage House, which served as the main entrance of our goal...The American Club. The high-peaked roofs of the Carriage House, designed to allow the masses of snow that would fall during the winter months to roll off to the ground, added to the stately air of the main entrance. A green-jacketed doorman welcomed us to Kohler and directed us to the front desk. The staff at the American Club turned out to be as professional as they were billed to be. A pretty young blonde girl behind the check-in desk let us know that a complimentary morning paper would be available in the lobby, but that if we wanted it delivered to our rooms we should just dial 55188 and it would be there within five minutes. She also let us know that at the end of the day the staff would provide an evening turndown service and a special bedtime dark German chocolate. We collected our keys as she highlighted the fact that each room was fully equipped with the best personal spa facilities produced by the Kohler Company. She wanted to make certain we knew that our rooms were a showcase of hot tub, shower massage, and tiled elegance that the Kohler Company is famous for. We each thanked her…I asked if she was on duty all night and was about to get an answer when Paul yanked me towards the door. “Come on,” he barked. “We got shit to do. You can try and mess around here later.” I gestured with my palms up in the air and winked. “Hope to see you later.” Her nametag said CLAIRE. She smiled. “Bye.”

Thirty-four

We stopped and asked the doorman if our directions were correct and hit the road once again. A short trip up Highway Y to county trunk FF led to the edge of Lake Michigan and the Whistling Straits course. On the horizon I could see twin stone chimneys which anchored each end of a rustic looking clubhouse. I looked at Paul and smiled. "This is going to be fricking great." He smiled back and nodded. It looked like he was a bit overwhelmed by the sight. "Can you believe we're actually going to be playing on the course which will host the 2004 PGA Championship?" I poked him in the ribs and said, "And none of the guys back at the office have been here yet. Not even that prick Scolcroft. That bastard gets to play the greatest courses almost everywhere he travels to. This is going to drive him nuts. I love it! He's gonna be sick with envy!"

Paul smiled back and nodded again. I think he was getting a grip on his emotions and with a look of contentment on his face he said, "Fuckin' awesome." As I focused on Paul's reaction, I began to reminisce again.

Thirty-five

The surge of memories was unstoppable, this time it was Paul and me. What a throwback to our days back at the University of Wisconsin. The two of us had been through many wild times together in college but we had lost track of each other for a few years after school and it was a crazy coincidence that we both ended up at QI. The biotech-testing giant had not always been the darling of the health care industry, so it was odd that we would both wind up there. I had started my drug career detailing for a good-sized drug company named Metaxa Pharmaceutical. I was responsible for the upper part of Wisconsin. I was having the time of my life as a sales rep detailing medicines in the great wintery northwoods. After two pretty good years with Metaxa my district manager figured out that I was spending more time drinking on Third Street in my old college party town than I spent calling on the doctors in my territory trying to sell Metaxa drugs. Realizing that I was about to be fired I began interviewing and moved on to Thor Inc. Thor was a much smaller drug company and didn't have much interest in background checks for their new hires. I was a warm body with drug sales experience. The Thor district manager was desperate and I was hired after just one interview. My career moved on again in a positive direction and I was just getting settled in as one of Thor's better reps when a small growth spurt in the business occurred and the company became hungry for experienced sales reps to promote to the level of district manager. I had convinced my regional manager, who was based out of Chicago, that I was just the guy to handle the Northern district in his region. At the time Thor had no large products to tout in the drug industry, and they had even less of a presence as a corporate identity in prescribing physician's minds. That all changed when Thor licensed in a product, that a competitor, Farnworth Pharmaceuticals Inc., thought would never make it as a big hit in the diabetes marketplace. Their mistake turned into a golden egg for Thor. The product was not only a hit, it turned out to be a revolutionary, best in class standard of therapy. After solid pre-promotion from the pumped up reps at Thor Inc. Glumosamide Sodium, trade named Glumax, hit the diabetic patient population like a force five hurricane. Clinical studies were published in most of the major medical journals. The studies showed that, in diabetes patients who had taken Glumax, there was a statistical significance in reduction of leg amputations, blindness and renal failure. These studies coupled with intense promotion from the Thor sales force skyrocketed Glumax sales to over two hundred million dollars in its first year. By the end of it's second year of sales Glumax was a bona fide billion-dollar product. Thor Pharmaceutical had hit the big time...and I was right there with them. This was all long before QI.

Thirty-six

But back at the beginning of my career, when I was still with Metaxa, Paul's career had moved in a different direction. He had been working as an operating room nurse at Lutheran Hospital in LaCrosse, Wisconsin. Our paths crossed again thanks to the healthcare industry. We had rekindled our college relationship immediately one winter day in the Lutheran Hospital Emergency Department. Paul was wheeling a car wreck patient down to the X-ray department when he stumbled onto me toting my alligator skin detail bag, the trademark of all Metaxa drug reps, down the hall. I was balancing a tray full of donuts when I saw him. Donuts were a requirement for entrée to the sanctum sanctorum of Lutheran...the doctor's lounge. After we hooked up again, Paul and I met regularly for breakfast on the days when I was working the docs at Lutheran. Our conversations ran from sports to politics to women. Our friendship was firming up just like in the days of old. It took me a couple of years to convince him to dump his lagging career as a male nurse, but he was finally ready. By the time he finally caved in and accepted a job with Metaxa, I had already moved on to Thor, Inc. Paul had been telling me that he was ready to jump to the commercial business side of medicine, and he was ecstatic that one of Metaxa's expansion divisions had an opening in the western part of Wisconsin. Paul interviewed for the position and he was hired. In his mind and in the minds of most of the health care industries too, Metaxa Pharmaceutical was a real winner. Paul wound up in the same Sioux Falls District I had been in and for a short time was teamed along with a superb group of detail reps. They all racked up trips to President's Club and then advancement opportunities began to come in. I had moved on to the North Carolina based home office of Thor. Paul had moved up at Metaxa and worked to become a superstar account manager in their professional Trade Relations group. Upon moving to QI I saw a need for industry professionals with trade experience as well as hospital knowledge and contacted Paul. He was brought into QI after a series of intense interviews and he proved that he would be to be a valued employee in short order. Paul's work experience in the hospitals had served him well. We corresponded frequently and partied at company meetings but did not get to actually work together too often. During the relatively rare times when business did bring us together, we committed to work hard but also wrap in as many rounds of golf as possible. Many a nineteenth hole was visited and we quaffed as many rounds of beer as we could stand following the play. Now here we were, back together again, near our old stomping grounds, getting ready to take on one of the greatest courses on the planet.

Thirty-seven

Paul and I sat in the bar at the Whistling Straights clubhouse waiting for Paul's clients to show up. The sight, the place, the atmosphere was overpowering. Black Wolf Run, the original golf track at Mr. Kohler's American Club had already become famous in the minds of most golf fanatics before it was chosen to host the 1998 Women's U.S. Open won by Se Ri Pak. 1998 was a banner year in women's golf. Pak, in her first major championship as an LPGA professional, went wire-to-wire to capture the McDonald's LPGA Championship title, becoming the first rookie since Liselotte Neumann to win a major as her first Tour victory. In her second major championship, Pak became the youngest player to win the U.S. Women's Open after a 20-hole playoff with Duke University amateur Jenny Chuasiriporn. Their 18-hole playoff ended in a tie and was followed by two holes of sudden-death. The 92-hole tournament was the longest in women's professional golf history. Se Ri Pak joined Juli Inkster as the only other LPGA player to capture two modern major championships in her rookie season. Counting on the success of Black Wolf Run Mr. Kohler, a true golf fanatic, commissioned Pete Dye to build a stunner of a course on the western shore of Lake Michigan and called the new track Whistling Straights. This course, with thirteen of eighteen holes along the lake, would become the terror of the Midwest. The Straights Course would host the 1999 PGA Club Pro Championship, gain notoriety, and move on to be selected as the 2004 venue for the PGA Championship. The 1999 CPC event was won by Jeff Freeman. This young man came to the blustery shores of Lake Michigan and became only the seventh player in history to win the PGA Club Professional Championship in his first attempt. The course was brutal. Freeman was the only player to break par for 72 holes at the challenging Whistling Straits course. After leaving the American Club and prior to our round we stopped in at the pub located on the second floor of the rustic, yet classic clubhouse. It was the perfect place to spend our pre-round warm-up. We chatted with one of the bartenders about the history of the major events held at the Straights. "I remember it well," a young man in a starched white shirt stated. "The 32nd PGA Club Professional Championship seemed like a ghost match. The event was a bit more than eerie." He smiled, then turned serious. "A thick fog crept across Lake Michigan midway through the final round on Sunday. The fog, dark gray and thick in nature caused play to be suspended." His hands moved in slow tempo, like waves on the Great Lakes. "Later darkness settled in and would force a fifth day of competition for 51 players. Freeman salvaged his final round and the Club Pro victory by chipping in for birdie from 35 feet on the 13th hole." He pointed to the spot on one of the course maps that lay on the polish bar top. Later, Jeff sank a six-foot birdie putt on the 16th hole, right here," he pointed to a different spot, "and that sealed it for him. The victory capped what would be a special year for the first CPC winner from California. Jeff Freeman has a key to this club for the rest of his life. Mr. Kohler was ecstatic. He knew that young Se Ri and Jeff had put Kohler, Black Wolf Run and Whistling Straights on the map."

Thirty-eight

Just then we heard a tap on the bar, turned and heard a bearded middle-aged man yell, "I love this kind of talk! Buy the house a round on me!"

"Yessir, Mr. Kohler!" The bartender spouted back. "Right away sir." Kohler looked over at us, "Not too early to have a little hair of the dog. Is it men?" We smiled broadly as he continued. "Sounds like you boys want to hear about the Straights, is that right?" We nodded as two more frosty mugs were plopped down in front of us. "Well," he began, "the honor of hosting the 2004 PGA only came after hurried talk by me and some of my cronies was initiated suggesting that this wonderful course be in the running for a Ryder Cup or for a U.S. Open. All this well placed talk prompted the PGA to move quickly and make it their showcase." Kohler grinned, "If I do say so myself, it was a brilliant stroke." I scratched my chin and admitted silently that it had been a masterful rise from a desolate stretch of Wisconsin tundra to the pinnacle of the Professional Golfers Association. Kohler put his hands on our shoulders and walked us outside with our beers. "Look at that big beautiful lake boys. What a sight!"

As we turned east toward Lake Michigan we caught sight of the vast blue body of water, both feared and loved by sailors everywhere. "Did you know that Lake Michigan earned the respect of a vast volume of water lovers because of the number of lives it has taken?" Kohler walked down a flight of rough hewn stone steps and retold stories of the *Edmund*

Fitzgerald, the *Honrable III* and the *Bastion*. All famous tales of disaster and glory, which surfaced whenever talk of the Lake came up. A cold chill ran down my spine as I watched Paul stroll down a dirt path towards the course. As I looked over the mystical sight I could smell thick lake air prior to it pouring into my lungs. The wind whistled. Flags out on the course snapped. Mysteries held on those timeless winds sparked my imagination, and I swore the chill down my back was accompanied by that nagging presence of rosewater aroma. Granny? I shook it off. Mr. Kohler suggested we head back on into the bar and we agreed. Sitting at one of the center rounds in the old, rough looking room Kohler asked us what our plans were. "Well," I said. "We have some customers meeting us here for a few rounds of golf and then we have an appointment with the Packers on Sunday. He laughed and said, "Well make sure you enjoy yourselves and spread the word!" He looked to the bartender and said. "Buy these boys another round. And another one tomorrow too!" With that he bid us farewell and walked down to the ground floor of the clubhouse.

Thirty-nine

Paul and I finished our beers, tipped the bartender generously and decided to survey the rest of the layout we would be attacking the next few hours and then again tomorrow. Outside we walked slowly taking in the full sight before us. On our left a high row of mounded sand dunes guarded our view of the newly finished Irish Course, the second track of eighteen built by Mr. Dye at Whistling Straights. We were scheduled to play the Irish tomorrow after a late breakfast at the club. Regarding the Irish Course, Dye had been quoted as saying that; "There's nothing in the United States that has the look and feel of this course." A sharp right turn around a massive grassy dune gave us another beautiful view of the bleak, haunted looking stone clubhouse at Whistling Straights. Three large flags stood stiff in the breeze directly in front of the entrance. One, the flag of the United States. Next to it the Irish flag. Then the flag of the State of Wisconsin. The three proud pieces of snapping nylon signaled that this would be a tough, windy day out on the links. The clubhouse was truly a Scottish looking work of architecture. Not nestled in a grove of magnolias and pines like many of the clubhouses down south. This clubhouse was stark and cold looking like a stone-age chopper thrust purposefully into the ground. In front of the clubhouse across the road from the flags lay a monstrous putting green. This vast green expanse, which taunted many a golfer, stood like a gateway to the wonderful course that lay behind it. At that precise moment a group of three young men, and one willowy lady, who all looked as if they were waiting to go off toward the Straights Course, were putting on the practice green together. Off to the right of the pale practice green a bunch of young men in white coveralls chatted and smoked cigarettes. I figured that most of them were caddies. I had heard that many came over from Ireland to take advantage of the chance to get a better education, but that also quite a few were home grown. During the summer months these young men worked as caddies and during the school year went on to the University of Wisconsin in Madison on scholarship. Looping bags at a place like Whistling Straights not only allowed them to play the great courses here in the area more often then they could ever afford to on their own, but also provided a generous income, at forty dollars cash a round plus tips. On a good weekend the best of them could get two rounds a day in and rack up at least twice their pay in tips. If the job they did out on the course was viewed as exceptional by the golfers, each would pay twenty to twenty five dollars for the round. This entire amount coming to the caddies in cash made for a great summer job. Business people were the best customers for the caddies since they were often on an expense account. Paul, his customers and I fit the bill for big marks. The caddie master whistled at the next two young men in line and had them grab our bags.

Forty

The old caddie master looked at us with serious eyes then smiled and said, "These are the best two laddies we have fellas. I hope you treat them right."

"We will," Paul smirked. "Have my guests shown up yet Pete?"

"Yeah, they been here at least an hour now. I think they were worried they might miss you somehow and blow their chance to play. They were over there putting for a while. Now I think they're out on the range. It's just over that mound." He pointed in the direction of the range. "Ian! Stu! Get these gents bags over to the range and warm them up. She's gonna be a cool one today. They'll need to be limber."

"Hey Paul, how did you know that guy? I thought you'd never been here before?" I asked.

"You didn't think that I would take a risk on bringing out my best two customers to a place like this and not be prepared did you? Besides a few weeks back I got inspired and decided to walk the layout. Just to see how it was coming along. I ran into Pete back there and even though I haven't seen him since, I have been keeping in touch with him over the phone. He's heard of QI and most of the boys have too since it is such a big company here as well as over in the U.K. I told them how much golf we play and what kind of entertaining we do and they gave me the first class tour of the place. I even got to meet our drinking buddy Mr. Kohler...even though he didn't let on back in the clubhouse. By the way tonight's dinner is on him. We'll get the best of the best in the bar and at the table."

"God, am I going to owe you big after this one." I said.

"Yeah," Paul responded, "just don't forget me when you're running this company. I know you're on the fast track. And I don't care how modest you act. Or how much you tell me your life is screwed up. I'm putting my money on you and the million-dollar line of b.s. you can throw around. I figure it's gotten you a long way from LaCrosse it should be able to carry you just a bit farther. Don't you think?"

"Maybe...just maybe," I said. "But for now I'm just going to whack the ball around on the best course on the planet. Then we can work on Augusta and Pebble."

The clubhouse was nice, but as is true in most of the great golf venues it was designed to not overshadow the course. The bar upstairs looked inviting to us once again. I knew we'd wind up there after the round for a few Black and Tans, so the temptation was resisted. At the check-in we hooked up with Paul's customers. They were two senior scientists from the Thorvald Clinic, one of the Midwest's largest health care provider chains. We shook hands and exchanged greetings. Denny Drake, Thorvald's VP of Pharmaceutical Purchasing, was actually one of the bench pharmacists back in the Thorvald Clinic Pharmacy I used to call on when I was a sales rep in Eau Claire. We had plenty in common to talk about. Frank Kerr, the fourth member of our golf party was a Wisconsin transplant from Montana. He worked as the Vice President of Operations for Thorvald's clinical business. I left Paul and the Thorvald men on the practice tee and walked into the clubhouse to settle up for the green fees and to pick up some goodies for our customers. After ponying up for four rounds of golf, I bought some new Titleist balls, a couple of pro shop gift certificates and headed out the back path down to the first tee box. An older fellow who sported a fair Irish accent and a pair of green corduroy plus fours asked if we were all there and then gave us the course rules. "Play ready golf, no out of bounds and listen to yer caddies." he said. Frank asked if they ever let carts out on the Straights Course since he had seen some heading over to the Irish. "No carts would ever be allowed out on the Straights Course. Not now...not ever." he said. "So tighten up yer laces and get ready to play the best course ya'll ever set foot on. Be off now, and listen to Ian and Stu. They're the sharpest two caddies we got here at the Straights! They'll loop all four of yer bags and gi' ya plenny of advice. And if you're wise ya'll listen to them too. If not y'll be in the drink or the dust more often then ya want on a gorgeous day like this." He smiled a million-dollar smile and sent us on our way.

Forty-one

The six of us trudged down a crushed gravel path towards Lake Michigan and immediately broke into a banter about what kind of game we would play and who would be matched against whom.

"Well", said Paul, "since Tom and I are the hosts here why don't we try to take you two on as a team and then we can do any kind of side bets we want after that. If it gets too lopsided we can make changes tomorrow. But stakes for today's team bet are drinks back at the clubhouse with tip included. Deal?"

Frank Kerr looked over at his counterpart Denny, laughed a choked kind of a snort and said, “You’re on. Denny we have our usual going, but don’t let that screw up our drinkin’ bill tonight! Got it!”

“Yeah, yeah.” said Drake. “Just use your three wood off the tee today and keep it in the fairway. Don’t try to keep up with these two. I know that they spend more time on golf courses than they do in their offices...especially Paul.” He looked over at my partner and laughed, “Shit, I don’t even think he has an office.” Drake winked at me and said, “Hope that doesn’t get him in any trouble Tommy. He is a pretty good account manager, even if he doesn’t let us win often enough.” I smiled at Paul and then looked back at Drake and Kerr and said; “If he doesn’t spend enough time on the golf course he knows I won’t invite him back to my member-guest tournament in North Carolina. And I know he won’t jeopardize that. So no...you haven't gotten him in any trouble at all. Let's get at it. OK?"

"Not so fast!" says Drake. "What kind of game are we gonna have? I'm a 10. Frank's a pretty good 14. We need to have more going on then just a bunch of drinks. How about it?"

Well, I hang around 6 so I'll give you 5 and Frank 9 and we'll play full trash...sandies, doads, greenies and audible woodies. OK?"

Paul smirked and said, "OK by us. But notice there aren't to many trees out here. It'll be tough to get an audible woodie! Buck a point?"

"Yeah that'll be fine." I said, then bent down and pushed one of the Straights' trademark black tees into the ground. The wind kicked up as I was pushing down on my new Titleist Pro V1 and before I straightened up I caught the distinct smell of rosewater again. I swore I felt Granny's presence right there on the tee box and it once again really shook me up.

Not now I thought. Wasn't that just a dream? Or maybe just a drunken vision? I shook my head violently and stood up quickly. Maybe too quickly. My hangover was wearing off, but a stream of bile made it just a bit too far up my throat. Paul, Frank and Drake took this to be something more than it was and Paul asked me if I was ok. I said I was. That it was just a little shiver. I was ready to go. Stepping back from my ball I took in for the first time the beauty of the first hole at Whistling Straits. This marvelous par four would be the green carpeted grass channel peppered with nasty looking bunkers that would lead us out to the holes, which hung on the cliffs over Lake Michigan. We could see the lake out over the horizon, but it was hard to believe that this was autumn in Wisconsin. It truly was a rare day. The sky was azure blue. The wind was cool, but mild. And we were so far away from any mass civilization that the simple sounds of pure nature were everywhere and astonishing. Stu, the young man with my bag told me to keep it to the right. I took my usual pre-shot deep breath, stepped back two paces, raised my driver over my head, stretched it back behind me until I felt my spine crackle pleasantly and then walked up to my ball. I stared down at that little white dimpled rock and eased a low and slow back swing, which paused ever so slightly at the top and whipsawed a long gentle draw two hundred and forty yards down the right middle of the fairway.

"Uh-oh." said Frank. "We're gonna have to work today Denny. Get your mind into it."

"I will, I will." Came the reply. "Just keep your end up and we'll be fine." Paul winked at me as I stepped off of the tee. He laced a low straight shot that bounded past mine by twenty yards.

"So much for customer golf." I chuckled. We were off.

The first hole turned out to be pretty routine for all four of us. Probably due to our anticipation of playing such a great track. We all swung our clubs within our game and walked off of the hole titled "Outward Bound" with four pars. The match was even up after one. Not much happened on the next few holes. Number two named "Cross Country" took us out toward the lake and aimed us at a power plant down south toward Sheboygan. The wind was gentle at this time of day and we all made par there too. Next came O'Man, then Glory and then Snake. All were great holes and we reveled in the moment. We were four men who appreciated the beauty of golf, and we were breathing it in. All in large measure. The sixth, "Gremlin's Ear" was aptly named for the huge pot bunker in front of the green on this wily par four. None of us left with less than bogey. It seemed that that nasty bunker had magnets in it pulling our little white golf balls in from which ever way they spun off the faces of our high priced irons. Then came "Shipwreck"...aahhh, I'll never forget "Shipwreck". One of those golf holes I would remember for the rest of my life. But more on that later.

After nine we were up one over our customers, and Paul asked me if we needed to change the bet.

"No frickin' way!" Denny hollered. I was sipping on a beer I picked up at the halfway station when he had overheard Paul ask me the question. "We're gonna whip your asses on the backside. We haven't even turned into the wind yet." Denny clapped a big hand on his caddies back and said, "My boy here tells me that you sissies ain't got a chance against us once we get past the sheep!" He barked out a larger than life laugh. "What about doubling the bet, you big shot corporate boys?" I chugged the last of my beer and said, "I'm ready...let's go finish this thing!"

I hit a perfect drive off of the tenth tee box. The shot needed to climb steadily out toward Lake Michigan with a slight draw, and then land on an elevated plateau, which would then require a short iron shot to a tricky green. All the others hit too far to the left and were in the shit. It didn't matter in the overall scheme of things because my approach shot landed eight feet in front of the hole and crawled in for a chip in eagle. Drake and Kerr threw their freshly purchased Whistling Straights golf caps on the ground and swore like a pair of alter boys out of earshot of the Father. Paul slapped my hand and said, "Let's crush these bastards." I just winked at him.

True to form after a great hole, I doubled bogeyed the next hole and my emotions went off like Mt. Vesuvius. I was boiling on the inside. On the outside I just looked severely pissed off. Thankfully Paul halved the hole with Denny. On the way to number 12, "Pop Up", he kicked me in the ass and told me to quit being a baby and play. I did. Another beautiful par three along the lake. One hundred thirty eight yards. All four of us were on the green with birdie putts and I was the only one to sink it, for score. Paul and I were two up with six to go. After "Cliffhanger", number thirteen, we turned south again, but this time we were dead into a north blowing wind. The brilliant day was beginning to take hold of our game and as we looked south over the dazzling lake, the sparse scattering of wooly sheep and the essence of links golf, we collectively held our breath. "God, I need a beer." Said Paul. Denny agreed and pulled four out of his bag. He had purchased the beer from a stunning young girl back at the back nine rest station. "Boys," Denny held his can high. "To a great day. No matter how it turns out!"

"BBBAAAAHHHHHH!!!!" yelled Paul trying to mimic one of the grazing sheep. "Yeeeeehaaahh!" came a cheer from the rest of us. The sheep all turned in a confused stare and wondered what on earth had inhabited their peaceful existence. Anything other than eating, mating and defecating was foreign to them. We marched on. Fifteen was brutal. A normally reasonable par four, but into the near gale wind that had popped up, it was nothing but work. The same came true on sixteen. On any given day we all could routinely make par here, but not today. Not with this wind. Having grown up in this part of the midwest I wondered what it would be like to play this course on a blustery slate gray October day with a slight mist coming down. I thought, deep, deep down inside that I couldn't break one hundred on a normal nasty fall day at Whistling Straights. But today the temperature was perfect for October, and we played on. "Pinched Nerve", number seventeen decided the match. A two hundred sixteen yard par three. Dead into that nasty north blowing wind. The left side of the green consisted of a forty-foot drop to a slip of Lake Michigan sand. This hole spelled disaster. Denny and Frank had pulled to within one stroke of Paul and myself. They had the honors, which did not excite either of them. Frank confidently walked up to the tee first. His shot landed in the lake about twenty yards left of the small strip of sand, which separated Lake Michigan from the eastern shore of the state of Wisconsin. Denny, feeling the pressure, pushed his shot to the right side of the hole, not an impossible putt for him to make, but not a very easy one either. Paul, my buddy, led our team off and bunted a low, short three wood stinger which bounded fifty yards in front of the green, hopped once...twice...and looked to be perfectly on track until it hit a damp spot in front of the green and stopped two feet off the putting surface. Not bad, but only about equal to where Denny lay. I stepped up. Breathed in twice...deeply. On the second inhalation I sensed that rosewater scent again and tried to shake it off. Not to be done. I closed my eyes, and a thought as clear as a bright morning sun flashing through a freshly opened pair of curtains hit me square in my pre-shot setup. Granny. "Focus." The image said. As stunning as a beacon from a Cape Hattaras light house the word blazed. "Focus." I opened my eyes. My three wood went back. Once again. Low and slow. At the top of my back swing, just as I was ready to roll my shoulders over and hit the hardest three wood that I had ever hit, I heard, or maybe just felt, the word..."Stop!"

I didn't think about it. I just did it. And that pause...that simple little pause...produced a super fluid move that resulted in a shot that

I could see even before I picked up my head. The sense. The muscular reaction. The click. The question..."Wow...did I really hit it that solid?" The follow through. The sight of the ball, high in the air, coursing toward the green...no the hole! Two bounces, start of a little backspin and stop. My ball hung on the left edge of the cup...not an ace, but a definite kick-in. Even Denny and Frank were screaming. Paul tackled me on the spot and I never even felt it. What a shot. What a feeling. God, I loved this game.

Forty-two

That night after dinner I strolled outside the hotel to walk off some of Mr. Kohler's meal, and the drinks we had won at the clubhouse. The food was excellent. The drink even better. But once again I probably had had too much. I wasn't out of control like back in the Falls, but I did have a pretty severe package working. I hoped I hadn't offended the customers. Paul, Frank, Denny and I got back to the American Club pretty late and we found that they had to put our guests up in the American Club's sister facility, the Inn on Woodlake. This was a beautiful, quiet addition to the main hotel and posed no problem to our friends since our time in the rooms would be minimal. Out the back of the Inn, was a huge severely undulating practice green next to a glassy pond. A sign off to the left of the practice green directed me to a three-mile exercise path and I was off on a pleasant little walk. I thought back on the day visualizing each and every shot when the THWACK! of a hickory shaft struck me above the knees. The pain was minimal, but the shock of being hit so suddenly, when I thought I was by myself, rattled me.

"What the hell!" I exclaimed. Spinning around I was faced with the shimmering image of Granny Wolters again. She was still clad in her plaid golf attire. And she was still swinging that damnable putter. "Looked to me like you had a nice day. At least from my vantage point."

"Yeah, but..." I began to say.

"Be quiet!" she yelled. "I'm not ready for you to talk yet. When I want to hear from you I'll let you know. 'Til then you just listen. And try...please try to think." The ghost paused and walked towards a birch tree that was about as big around as she was, nearly thirty four inches in diameter. "First...have you called home to check on the boys? If not, why not?" I looked down at my feet in mild embarrassment. "No, I didn't have time." I said. "The clients were waiting and Paul and I had to take care of business." Granny raised that damnable putter again, started to swing, but stopped. She continued, "Let me clue you in on something. Your oldest, right now, is experimenting with his first sexual encounter with a girl." She glared at me. "Have you talked to him about the facts of life?" I reddened. "Hope so." she said. "If not you, and he could be sorry. I'm not sure you're ready to be a grandparent." The club came down in a vicious arc and poked me in the chest. Her putter was like William Tell's arrow...in search of my soul. "Second...have you thought about what I told you back in the Falls? I know you were a bit whacked out, but what I said wasn't that much, and it certainly wasn't that hard. Even a sot like you should have been able to grasp it." I shook my head and wished I hadn't drunk so much back at the bar. That damn hard liquor had to go. She continued the lecture. The fire in her eyes was different than anything I had ever seen. I could feel the love that she always had for me deep in my breast, but I knew that I had best just shut up and listen. "I told you to always just trust yourself. Play life like you play a course. If you lived your life like you played today you'd be in great shape. Remember when I said to have confidence in yourself?" I nodded. "If you have that kind of confidence you'll make any shot you want.

That goes for life too. You can have the best this life has to offer just because of that trust in yourself. You can succeed at anything with a free swingin' kind of shotmakin' confidence. Even if you screw up once in awhile, and you probably will, just keep playin' on. If you screw up and don't recover so well, well then just hike your trousers up and learn from it." The wispy image turned. She walked back and forth...to and fro...swinging the putter...I could see the frustration pulsating off of the ghostly vision in waves. Suddenly she turned and with another one of those looks capped in love and fire she hollered, "Think about how you laced that first drive out into the fairway on Number One! You didn't even realize you were hitting a golf ball did you?" She paused, "Did you!" I shook my head. "You were thinking about what a nice day it was. How beautiful Lake Michigan looked. You were wondering what was ahead of you out on this exciting new course. You didn't know what was out there, but you were excited about it. Looked forward to it. You were eager, happy, confident." I looked up at the woman who had taught me all that I needed to know about playing golf and realized for the first time that she had also been teaching me all that I needed to know about life. She continued, "You played along marvelously until the seventh hole." I put my head in my hands. "You remember, it was called 'Shipwreck' the second tough par three along the lake. One hundred ninety two yards of sheer terror. All of a sudden the lake wasn't beautiful anymore. This Wisconsin Indian Summer Day had begun to turn sour in your mind. It was a menace. Clawing at you. Begging you to throw the ball hard to the right into the waiting icy depths of Lake Michigan. Come join the Andrea Doria...come sink with me. Something...some kind of obstacle was out there trying to pull you down. Trying to stop you short. Trying to wreck your day." My thoughts, as I gripped my temples, went back to that hole. I was cruising along smoothly, playing my heart out, relaxed, smooth, confident...but Granny was right. Doubts did pop up. Where had they come from? There was no reason for me to derail. Granny snapped back at me, "But what did you do? Did you let it get to you? Did you sit down and pity yourself for having to face such a brutal obstacle? No! You stepped right up to that monster, focused on your two best swing thoughts and laid down the prettiest little fade this course has seen to date." I had hit a great shot onto that green. "Shipwreck" would always be a hole that I would remember. A hole I would refer back to. Granny poked me in the chest again, "What if you handled your personal life the same way?' Whoa...I thought...where did this come from? This wasn't golf. She continued. “It would not only help you conquer your inner fears, but it would be great for those kids of yours to see their Dad swinging hard with confidence rather than runnin’ scared with his indecisive tail between his legs.” She poked me with the putter again. Not quite so hard this time. “Now get back to that hotel and give those kids a call. Ask them questions. Find out what they did today. Don’t tell them what you did. Don’t tell them things...things won’t do them any good right now. Knowing that you are interested in them will. Now git!” THAWACK! I ducked as the hickory shaft came down again and when I looked up, she was gone. A short echo rang in my ear as I scanned the dim green forest for any sign of her...“Use your mistakes to make you better. Not worse. Not worse. Not worse...”

“Uh”,...I finally spoke. But after that, nothing came out of my mouth. I shook my head and stumbled a few feet down the path trying to put together what had just happened. I hurt. Both mentally and physically. I was lost. Befuddled. Stunned and scared. Was the ghost of my dear old dead Granny really visiting me? It couldn't be, but this was the second time I had actually seen her. How could this be happening? Once again I confirmed that I did not believe in the supernatural. Even if she wasn't real, the things she was saying were so right on the money. She always was there to straighten me out when I was a kid...why not now? I stopped. Walked back two steps. Forward three. She was dead that's why...but what was death anyway? I always felt death was just the next stage in life. Not necessarily the end of everything, just another phase, another shade. Maybe that's what she was, yeah...a shade, showing up when I needed her most. When I needed some guidance, some advice. Maybe it wasn't a ghost; maybe it was just my common sense kicking in. "Yeah," I said out loud, this time it was not just in my head. "It wasn't a ghost. It was just my common sense." I turned to walk back to the hotel and fell flat on my face on the path. I cursed, and as I dusted myself off I realized I had tripped over a single sprawling root of a hickory tree that looked strangely familiar, kind of like the shaft of an old putter.

Forty-three

Back at the American Club I walked into the dimly lit lobby and prepared to give the boys a call. Granny, the shade, or whatever it was, twanged my guilty conscience enough to sting a leather-skinned mule. Before I got to the staircase, a familiar voice yanked at me.

"Hey Tom!" Paul called out from the club's bar. "Come on in and have a nightcap!" Guilt tugged at me as I began to wave him off. I walked past the front desk and noticed the pretty young blonde who had checked us in earlier in the day. She smiled and said, "Oh Mr. Wolters I have two notes for you. I reached for them. She pulled back just a bit and then thrust forward to give them to me. Her hand lingered in my palm. She dropped two sealed envelopes into my outstretched fingers. As I walked to the elevator I read the messages. The first was from home. The neighbors had called to let me know that all was well with the boys. Josh was spending the night with friends and Eric was already home eating pizza and watching a movie. The second simply said: I'm off at ten, meet me in the bar. Hmmm...I thought. The desk girl? If so it would be worth the trip. I took a U-turn and met Paul in the club's bar. He looked up and said, "Yes! I knew you wouldn't fold on me." I grinned and pushed the relatively short responsible side of my personality out of the way and succumbed to the offer of more alcohol. My scrambled brain told me that one or two more short ones couldn't hurt. I had had a rough day. A confusing day. And besides, it was early,

Josh was out and Eric would be okay until tomorrow when I could give him a call. I sat down. Time slipped away. At midnight came the word from the barkeep.

"Last call fellas." The young man said, "One more round?"

"Yeah, what the hell. Might as well polish the night off on a good note." I looked at Paul through a single malt mist and wondered where the night had gone. I also wondered why my ten o'clock partner had not shown up. No one had ever come to the bar asking for me. At least I didn't think anyone had. I looked over at Paul, "Hey…I had quite a shot on number eight today dinnit I?"

"Eat crap." Paul blurted back a bit louder than necessary. "That was the luckiest frickin' thing I've seen in months. You suck!"

"Yeah…yeah." That was the wittiest comeback I could fling back in my current state. Time to go. I signed the bill off to my room and staggered out of the bar. I bounced down a narrow hallway in the general direction of my room. At the end of the hall was a full-length mirror. I looked up into it and there, standing behind me at the other end of the hall, was that wispy image of Granny again. She was shaking her head while she twirled that damn hickory-shafted putter. She stopped it in mid twirl and pointed it directly at me. I spun around to tell her to get lost, but when I did there was nothing there. After a short desperate search going up two...or maybe three different hallways, I found my room. I fumbled a bit with the key, but finally got the door open. The sound of water, running in the exquisite Kohler outfitted bathroom, piqued my curiosity. Had I left something running? Maybe it was the maid. Then, I spied a pile of women's clothing bunched on a chair next to the door, which led to the bath. I edged the door open and gazed at the figure of the young desk clerk standing naked in the shower adjusting all of the jet spray shower heads strategically so the cascading water covered up most of the delicate parts of her anatomy. She cracked open the door, smiled and curled her index finger at me indicating that I needed to come on in. I quickly shed my clothes, climbed into the shower and helped with the shower head adjustments. After she left, I spent the rest of the night in a fitful tossing and turning type of sleep that assured general fatigue the next day. Only one part of my body slept peacefully. It was spent.

Forty-four

I woke up to a blaring alarm at 7:00 am and decided I had better get with it and call my boys. The chances of me getting them before they were off to one of their friends' houses were pretty good if I could catch them early enough. Then I remembered that Josh wouldn't be home. Maybe I could catch Eric. The phone rang fifteen times before I finally hung up. I wasn't sure why the answering machine didn't click on, but the queasy stale alcohol feeling in my stomach was not helped by the situation at all. I showered, got dressed and went down to the lower lobby.

At breakfast, Paul looked at my bloodshot eyes with a pair of his own.

"Good thing we have a late tee time today." He reached across the table for a crock of strawberry jelly and dumped a knife full of it onto a large piece of whole-wheat toast. "I can't wait to see what the Irish Course has in store for us. I don't think it will be as tough as the Straights, but it is supposed to be a classic in it's own right." Between bites of scrambled eggs loaded with melted cheddar cheese and near-burnt hash brown potatoes Paul kept rambling about what had transpired the day before. My mind was on my lack of discipline, my concern for the situation at home and a dull sort of curiosity about my night visitor, who was not at the front desk this morning. I also was fighting down a sledgehammer thud of a hangover. We finished breakfast, both wanted to stop back at our rooms, and agreed to meet back in the lobby around ten o'clock.

Paul called Frank and Denny and told them that they were to meet us in the lobby at ten too. They told Paul that they were ready to take on the Irish and would surely be there at nine fifty nine on the dot. At the prescribed time, I closed the door to my room and took off for the hotel lobby. The lobby was nearly empty due to the late morning hour. Most of the club's activity took place in the early morning or after the afternoon round. Paul and I rounded the corner near the registration desk and we found our playing partners sitting in one of the small reading rooms located off of the lobby's main hallway. Frank looked up over a copy of the Milwaukee Journal-Sentinel and asked how we were doing.

"Fine," I mumbled. "Just fine."

"You both look like shit." Denny poked Frank in the ribs and laughed, "I think we're gonna get 'em today partner. I knew that the temptation of one last round would take care of Tommy. You can tell a guy who doesn't know when to quit from a mile off." I frowned as Denny continued. "And he's one of 'em." Frank smirked and asked if we still wanted to double the bet. I looked over at Paul and winked. "Sure. That is if you saps figure that a little 'ole hangover is gonna stop me from crackin' The Irish Course today." Fighting the bile rising in my throat I said, "I will certainly be happy to relieve you of more of your cash." I looked at my partner and said, "And I bet Paul will stand up to some of the action too. What do you say podgee?" Paul nodded in agreement. Podgee was my personal slang for partner. I don't know where it came from. Probably one of my South Carolina buddies on a Myrtle Beach trip. But Podgee was a true term of endearment. A compliment to the link between two golfing buddies.

"I'm in." Paul said as he glanced at the morning paper's headlines. "Hey did any of you guys buy any of this Mantera Bisco stock?"

"I got some when it first came out," said Frank. "Why."

"They just caught the CFO with his hand in the cookie jar. Could be trouble for the whole industry."

Frank seemed to blanche a little bit, "These CEO's are getting a bit out of control. Enron, Tyco, all of the dot com madness. Too bad just a few bad apples makes the whole business community look like a band of gangsters."

"Sorry," Paul said changing the subject. "I don't want to get the day off to a bad start, but that's what I get for not reading only the sports page like I'm supposed to." Paul scratched his head, "Wonder if State beat Carolina? That's the important shit. I gotta quit going to the business page first." I spoke up, "Come on boys, the car is out front, the clubs are waiting at the driving range, let's go play!

Forty-five

We pulled back up to the awe inspiring clubhouse an hour prior to our 11:45 tee time. Since the initial excitement of being at this wonderful golf venue had begun to change from anticipation to strong desire to let's start playing. We all went to the driving range. Upon arriving at the broad expanse of golf ball littered land, we saw that our caddies, the same two as yesterday, were already waiting with our bags. The banter was sparse as we stretched, swung handfuls of clubs, checked new golf balls and pulled on fresh golf gloves.

The caddie master grinned largely at us and said, "Off you go boys. And don't forget the big tip!"

The Irish Course was the second stretch of holes at the Whistling Straights track. With more than a hint of the Emerald Isle in its style and personality, the Irish Course at Whistling Straits possessed all the character of a centuries' old legend. As much as our group enjoyed the Straights Course the day before, we could hardly contain ourselves since this new course had only been open two weeks. We would be four of just a handful of golfers on the planet to have played this soon to be legendary eighteen. Our caddies took turns spouting the guidebook jargon regarding the newest addition to Whistling Straights. Stu began, "The Irish Course completes 72 holes of the most diverse golf experience in the world. The course is another Pete Dye masterpiece and a perfect companion to the adjacent, stunning Straits Course." The boy must have memorized this line because it was coming out in an enthusiastic but canned manner. "Tranquil grasslands. Soaring dunes. Cavernous bunkers. And, to ensure that golfers will remember the Irish Course, Dye claims he has used "every trick I've ever learned" in routing and sculpting the hole dynamics." "Oh come on boys," I said. "Remember us from yesterday? You don't have to give us the big speech. We're sold already." I winked at my companions. "Let's go play."

Even though this round was supposed to be more competitive than the day before at the Straights course all four of us got wrapped up in the beauty Pete Dye and the hand of God had created. Dye had made the most out of the endlessly fickle personality of nearby Lake Michigan. It was masterful how he had provided intriguing prospects at every turn. There were decisions to be made everywhere. Potential disaster, or ultimate joy. Should you try to carry the creek on number 9, or lay up short? Would it be smart to steer clear of a group of 40-foot bunkers on the right at hole number 13, or fall victim to the wetlands on the left of this "blind" par three?

We walked out onto The Irish Course with Ian and Stu for round two of our match. Even though this course layout was positioned inland from the Straights we were informed that it had ten bridges crossing over four streams that meandered through the property. And thankful we were that the track still offered panoramic views of Lake Michigan from several of the most challenging holes. Stu caught up to me prior to getting to the first tee box and said, "Mr. Wolters, every hole on this course will inspire you to play your best golf. Every stroke you take will challenge your talent and your knowledge of the game." I pushed back my hat and said, "Stu, you're starting to sound like that damn guide book again." He laughed and said he would stop. "You know the old saw...Keep up...Put up...and Shut up!" I was committed to enjoy this round of golf even while pounding our opponents into the ground. I would play easy, swing easy, just like Granny had coached me.

Hole Number One demanded a tee shot that needed to favor the right side of the fairway in order to allow for a better approach to the green. After our fairway shots, Paul and I lay side by side right in the perfect spot for an easy approach. Denny and Frank, still smarting from their day on the Straights dug deep and matched our efforts. Deep bunkers short and left made our position on the right the safe approach. We all played an extra club on our approach shots to compensate for a pesky hill, which led to an elevated green. Paul and Denny made their putts for birdie. Frank and I each missed ours. First hole all square.

We halved number two in a similar fashion. All four of us knocked three woods off the tee to the right side of the fairway where there was plenty of room to avoid what would have to be a massive carry over water down the left side. The approach posed little problem, but the tricky green caused us all to two putt. Still even after two holes.

Hole number three left us shaking our heads after we all three putted on this nearly impossible green.

Four showed us a partially hidden fairway, craggy grass, and plenty of dunes to maneuver around. Frank tried to cut too much of the dogleg left angle and left Paul and I an opening to go one up. Denny began barking at Frank while my podgee and I slapped hands.

The second shot on five took us across the first of the nasty little creeks, which would lace through most of the rest of the course. A tough hole, called “Devil’s Elbow”, it played nearly 520 yards much of it into the wind.

The best option was to stay left off the tee, then lay up short of the creek on the second shot. I was feeling pretty good about my three-wood this day and safely pounded my approach over the creek landing onto a knobby strip which made for a very narrow opening to the green. I was sitting on an uneven lie across the creek, but chipped up nicely with my sixty-degree wedge and tapped in a natural birdie. Paul and I pulled ahead.

Seven didn’t offer too much trouble in spite of the resident “troll” which supposedly guarded this hole. Eight only prepared us a tiny bit for number nine. Our team was still up one at this finishing hole of the front nine. If we were playing from the back tee, which we weren’t thank goodness (but the pros would be in 2004), any attempt at carrying the creek would require at least a three hundred-yard cannon shot. Maybe some of the tour boys could pull it off but we all decided to play it short of the creek. This left us with a two hundred-yard approach to a deep green. We needed to carry all two hundred yards as all the danger lurked in front of this green which sloped forward at the front lip and toward the back, but held an ugly knob in the middle. Without regard to Ian and Stu's advice, we all went for the green. Paul made it. Denny went right into some sandy scrub. Frank and I dumped our shots in the creek. Denny lofted a wedge out of the sand directly into the hole. A miraculous shot which unnerved Paul who missed a shaky four footer. All even after nine.

We all opted for stopping at the clubhouse for a quick beer and to take a leak. I was out first waiting on an order of four bottles of

Harp's when Granny made her first appearance of the day.

"Now...here ya go drinkin' agin. Ain't you ever gonna get enough of that stuff?" I rubbed my gloved hand over my face and tried to shoo her away. "There's some boys that are gonna be needin' you soon. Are you gonna be ready to help when the time comes?"

"Hey Tom! Come on. Where's the beer?" yelled Paul.

I turned back to grab the four bottles from the cart girl and felt no presence of Granny. Good I thought to myself. Good riddance.

Only three holes mad any impact on the back side of this fantastic tract of land which lived up to every bit of it's billing as the Straights very capable sister course.

Ian looked over at me and said, "Pay no attention to your pin sheet! I'll be your eyes here. This here green is huge, over fourteen thousand square feet. And even though you can't see it, you should be ok." Stu chimed in not to be outdone by his caddying partner, "From the upper tees, where you'll be hittin' from, play one club less. It's mostly a blind approach. But there's a lot to the hidden portions of the green. Just avoid the creek on the left and you'll be ok." The hole was playing about one hundred sixty yards so I pulled out a seven iron and stroked a towering shot that soared high into the crisp lake air and disappeared from view as it landed somewhere down where the green had to be. "Yer gonna love that one Mr. W." Ian said following a low whistle. "I hope you got some cash handy. That's right on line with the hole."

Paul and Frank hit smooth shots too, but they both seemed a bit off line. Denny waggled his seven iron, which may have been just a bit of a stretch for his game, and let off a high hook which was destined for the creek on the left. "Oh, too bad sir." Ian said. "That one's bound to be wet." Sure enough we heard the click of the ball a few seconds after it disappeared from view toward the creek. It sounded as if it hit on some rocks or something equally hard. As we anxiously walked down the sharp slope to the green thoughts of "Ace" danced in our heads due to the fact that the full green was coming into view and only two balls could be seen. Obviously they belonged to Paul and Frank. Denny was in the creek. I felt that "Blind Man's Bluff", hole number 13 at the Irish Course, Whistling Straights, was my lucky hole. The stunned look on Ian's face as he drew back from the flagstick was nothing compared to the shock of the group a few moments later when it was discovered that not only was my ball in the hole...but Denny's was too! The only explanation was that his ball had hit a rock, bounded into the air, and odds against all odds either landed in directly or bounced toward and rolled into the already occupied hole. "A DOUBLE ACE!" Paul screamed. "This is gonna generate bar talk for years." Our group nearly stumbled through fourteen, fifteen and sixteen, but when faced with two of the toughest closing holes we would see here on the west coast of Lake Michigan our senses came back into check. We wanted to continue to soak up every bit, every memory, of this wonderful course, on this exceptional day.

"Irish Mist", Number17, offered up a tee shot which severely tested our nerves. Ian and Stu came to our rescue once again by suggesting that we use an iron or fairway wood off the tee. "Time to be intelligent sirs," Stu said. "Water guards the entire left side of the fairway and fronts the green. You're gonna face dunes all down the right side." Pointing at their location he continued, "They are as intimidating as anything out here, although there is more room than you can see. Trust me on this shot. After the tee ball, play enough club, make sure it's one you have confidence in, to carry you onto the green." He turned and faced us. "It's very narrow and has a bump in the front and another one in the middle. The stick is between 'em." As our foursome looked down the fairway at the distant green, the dark water on the left seemed to call to us. The dunes on the right spelled certain bogey, if not double. The wind was picking up and the match was still tied. I whispered to myself, "Time to produce."

I picked up my five wood, a Steelhead, and walked up the tee box. I stuck a black tee in the ground and breathed in slowly. Just like always...set up...tighten stomach muscles...breath...low and slow. The ball ripped down the middle of the fairway. I new that if it had eyes it would have grinned left towards the water, then right as it sailed past the deadly dunes. On it's decent it bounded down in the middle of the fairway, leapt forward propelled by topspin and came to a soft spot a healthy two hundred thirty plus yards in front of where I stood. The rest of the group played safe too. But I had to wait until after they had hit to make my approach. I was a scant one hundred twenty five yards from the pin. I was reminded by Stu to take enough club, so I opted for an eight iron even though I felt I could get a nine there. The shot was hit flush on the face so I knew it would be long. The ball hit the back of the green with a ripping force. Backspinning wildly the ball bit into the green and spun like a yo-yo on a tight string back toward the second of the large mounds on the green. The ball reached the apex of the mound just as it ran out of steam and then ever so slowly crept up over the top and down the front side of the mound stopping four inches from the waiting pin. An easy birdie for me won the hole and put our team up by one with one to go. We couldn't lose the match, but we wanted desperately to win it outright. Paul gave me the thumb's up and pointed silently to the eighteenth tee box.

Forty-six

"If you want to see where to hit your lay-up second shot, keep your tee shot left. Your skills will be tested, as the left side requires a long carry over water and a bunker. A second shot lay-up, which carries the creek, leaves a short but blind uphill approach. A lay-up short of the creek leaves a longer approach to an elevated yet visible green. Aim for the center of the green, as there is a large, deep bunker left and the green drops steeply to the right. Missing the green on either side will cost you more than a "black and tan" in the Irish Pub after playing this very difficult finishing hole." Stu smiled as he finished reading the description straight from the yardage book and said, "Got that Mr. W? You needed the straight scoop. Right from the book. This is a tough one." It turned out he was right, but we wound up halving the hole and winning the match. Number seventeen had been Paul's and my lucky number. "Come on boys." I yelled after picking my ball out of the eighteenth hole. "The bar is thissa way!"

Forty-seven

"Good God." I whispered as my hands shot up to block the first morning light out of my blood red eyes. I was never going to learn. The normally cool, crisp sheets in the hotel bed were clammy and twisted around my legs like a cotton squid longing to drag me further down to the bottom of an alcohol ocean. Another night at the bar. Another morning in hell. Just what the doctor ordered. I decided to get in touch with my shrink. I questioned myself. Why could I know, and agree with everything that Dr. LaFleur had been telling me, and yet still keep throwing myself into this never-ending cycle of self-destruction? The light on my cell phone blinked red indicating that someone had tried to get hold of me. Maybe it was LaFleur having a premonition that I was in need of help. I turned toward the right side of the bed and saw that the light on the hotel phone was blinking madly too. I couldn't get up the intestinal fortitude to listen to anyone just now. I needed a long hot shower...and then an even longer cold shower. Then and only then would I give the good doctor a call and get my head straight. Thank God for the Kohler family. I was in the perfect place for the type of water massacre my body needed. I knew that if I could just make it to the bathroom I could get into the room's first class shower, which had been so entertaining two night's before, and just sit until the blaring light of reality dimmed enough for me to face the real world. I began to make a wobbly move to the waiting shower. I thought of those cool, smooth tiles beckoning me to them. I began to feel them on the hot soles of my feet. On the tired ache of my back. Just being able to lay my rough, bearded face on those tiles would bring me back. I got in and turned the water on. I don't know why, but a sudden, strange thought struck me. I decided to pray. I couldn't muster the strength to talk out loud so I thought the prayer out in my soggy brain. "Dear God forgive me for my sins." I began. "I know they are many. I guess you know that too. Bless everyone and everything everywhere. Bless Eric as he gets ready to end this current stage of his life...high school. Bless him as he prepares to enter the next great stage of life for a young adult...the college years." I paused and cranked the handle of the multi-shower a bit more to the HOT side. The blast sparked my senses. I continued. "Bless Josh as he moves into the age of responsibilty...sixteen. Sixteen years old.

Ready to drive. Not ready to be on his own. Yet thinking he is more than old enough. Bless this wild child that I have neglected for so long." I stopped and took a deep, rough breath. The water continued to pour down on me like a cleansing torrent of guilt as I once again fell into unconsciousness.

Forty-eight

The ringing brought me to. The God Damned ringing. My damp face felt like lead on my pillow. Somehow I must have made it back to the bed. I couldn't remember how. I reached for the phone and fumbled it before I got it up to my ear.

"Mr. Wolters?"

"Yes."

"This is the Wake County Sheriff's Office. I have some bad news sir...are you sitting down?...sir?"

"Yeah, Yeah I'm sitting down. What's up?"

"I'm sorry to be the one to tell you this sir, but it's about your son, your son Josh has been in an accident. He's dead." Now I had finally hit bottom.

Forty-nine

Sitting in the oversized brown leather seat in an old but comfortable Midwest Express jet my brain sizzled. The blur that was the day before seemed to never end. I do recall that following the phone call I blanked. I'm still not sure if I drank myself to a stupor or was just in a state of catatonia. But I did blank. For several hours. I began to come around after Paul had poured some strong black Starbuck's down my throat and turned the icy water jets on my slack body again and again. Then the anger surfaced. An anger filled with guilt. Frosted with remorse and lit with the candles of bereavement. God I needed to get home. I began to chatter about making arrangements and Paul in his wisdom just let me go until the moment I stopped cold in my tracks and began to cry. I crumpled into my old friends shoulder and just let the agony pour from my soul. My child. My ex-wife. My self doubts. My fears. All collapsed in on me in a torrent of crushing emotional streams culminating in a sea of self-pity and longing for that island in the middle of the sea called second chance. Paul gave me a couple of Valium tablets that he always had on hand for back spasms and tucked me into the freshly made-up hotel bed. I slept. And then I began to dream. The dream was one of those reality types, crystal clear and familiar, but still a dream.

Fifty

The cry in the middle of the night woke me up. I rolled over and saw Mary gently snoring curled up in the fetal position. What the hell I thought, she needs the rest. My feet were tangled up in the sheets and I nearly fell flat on my face trying to get out of bed, but I made it with an elegant stumble. The night was pitch black. I groped for the bureau that stood on my side of the bedroom. As I passed by it my hand lightly touched my watch, my glasses and my wedding ring. I slowly fingered the ring and turned back to look at Mary. The darkness prohibited my seeing her, but I could feel her there. So quiet. So peaceful. My God I thought, thank goodness I didn't screw this marriage up. Sure we still had our bumps in the road, but we were still together. Now with our second child, Josh, our marriage had finally solidified. At least I felt it had. Mary and I never really talked about our situation. Our love for each other. We just felt comfortable being together and living each day as it came. We knew that we didn't need to get all gushy about it. It just was. I walked past Eric's room and briefly looked in. He was sleeping like an angel. As always. I stroked his long blonde hair. Josh's cry started to become a scream and I hurried to his crib to pick him up. The feel of carrying a little baby is probably the greatest gift life has to offer, even when the little bugger is crying. I had felt that way with Eric, and now I was experiencing it again with Josh. Downstairs in the kitchen I pulled a pre-mixed bottle out of the refrigerator and set an enamel pot half filled with water on one of our stove's gas burners to warm up. I had nearly perfected the timing of heating a bottle, even in the dead of night. Josh had stopped crying when I picked him up from his crib, but now down here in the kitchen he was getting antsy again. I stuck a Nuk pacifier in his mouth to keep him occupied while the formula warmed up. The pantry just off of our kitchen doubled as a small sitting room because an old wooden rocking chair that had been passed down in our family for decades fit nicely in there. I gently sat down in the rocker and began to lean back and forth when the aroma of stench invaded my nostrils. Josh wasn't just hungry...he was loaded to the brim. I got him cleaned up with a new diaper and plenty of baby powder and was about to sit back down when my internal timer told me that the formula was probably the perfect temperature. It was.

The bottle took its place in Josh's mouth as soon as the pacifier came out. He cooed gently and began to drain the bottle. The rocking, the warmth of him lying on my chest and the darkness all converged on me and I became woozy. Once again I detected a slight aroma. But this time it was the smell of rosewater. I figured I was just dreaming (not knowing that I really was) and tried to ignore it.

"Hey." A small whisper in my ear tugged at me. "Hey, Tommy boy, wake up. I gotta talk to you."

I turned my head from side to side cracking my vertebrae in a way that actually sounded horrible but felt pretty good. I had just about regained my light doze when something hard, probably made of metal tapped me on the head. I started, but was careful to not wake the baby. My eyes tried to focus in the dim light of the pantry but couldn't quite make out who or what was rapping me in the head.

"Tommy, you awake yet?" a familiar yet distant voice whispered to me. "Or do I hafta whack you a bit harder?" I heard a small cackle of laughter after the metal object rubbed me behind the ear a bit more firmly than I liked.

"What the hell is going on?" I muttered. "Who is that? And quit hitting me with that spoon."

"This ain't no spoon Tommy boy." The voice said. "A spoon is for out in the fairway. This here is a niblick. Actually a mashie niblick and if you don't pop up out of that doze and talk to me I mean to mash you somethin' fierce. Now git up!" The voice raised up an octave and I responded.

"Granny?" I wondered out loud. "Is that you?" I held Josh with my left arm and rubbed at my eyes. It looked like her and smelled like her but I couldn't quite get the cloudy shimmer to leave the edges of her body. It seemed like she was standing in a fog made dull by the light of a half moon.

“Yeah…it’s me,” she said. “My God isn’t that the prettiest little baby you ever seen in your whole life? How could you ask for more of a blessing than a little gift like that?”

“Granny you’ve been dead for years. How can you be here?”

She cackled a little bit again and said, “Don’t you worry about how I got here. I just need to give you a bit more advice and I don’t want you to shut my words out because you don’t believe in spirits or ghosts or whatever you want to call those of us that have passed on to the next world.”

She stood over me at a bit of a right angle and appeared to be stroking the top of Josh’s head with her hand. Or what I thought was her hand anyway.

“This one’s special Tommy boy”, she said. “I don’t think I’ve seen a more special one since

I held you so long ago." She paused for a moment, crossed her arms over her brown checkered cardigan and said, "You know as a matter of fact it was in that very chair that I first rocked you to sleep when you were a babe. It was in that very chair that I would rock you until you were too big to be rocked anymore." She seemed to grow pensive again. "Don't lose that feeling Tommy boy. Even after that little bundle gets up and walks away from you."

"Awe Granny. This little bugger will be here forever." I arched my back to take the ache out of it. "I can't wait until this one gets up and starts moving around on his own. All he does now is fidget and squirm. It's all he's done since he came home from the hospital." My thoughts turned to the times Mary and I argued who would hold little Josh next. He was such a handful.

"Be careful of what you ask for Tommy boy", Granny mused. "He could be gone quicker than you think."

"That'll be the day." I said. "As peaceful as he is now most of the rest of the day this one is go, go, go. I can't wait 'til he's gone. At least out of my arms. Then my back will stop aching."

"Ok, ok", she said. "I know that's how you feel now, but just try to hold on to the feeling you have right now. Cherish it. Memorize it. Never let it go. Even when you decide to let him go. "Or," she looked at me with an overtly sad expression, "or when he's taken away from you." I cringed in the rocker as a cold breeze blew down my neck making the ache in my back worse.

"But don't you worry Tommy boy!" the cackle back in her laugh. "I'll never let this one wander about alone. I'll always be there to show him around the course. Just like I did for you."

The hazy fog began to disappear from view in spite of how hard I tried to keep her in my vision, she was gone. All I could hear was the clack of her mashie niblick on the floor in front of me. Somewhere out there.

My neck hurt fiercely as I rose up out of the dream. The flight attendant had asked us to prepare for landing in Raleigh-Durham. We would be on the ground in ten minutes. The dream lingered in my mind. The force of my grief began to surge again, but my desire to remember Granny's words quelled the emotional wave. I actually thought I felt Josh in my arms as the leather chair in the Boeing 707 became an old rocker in my mind's eye.

Fifty-one

The funeral was nothing special. Just another funeral. Except that it was the funeral of my little boy. My Josh. My collegues and friends from QI were there. To my surprise even Mary showed up with her husband and the twins. I sat alone in the first pew with Eric. The priest said all the right words. The music was beautiful. I cried at all the right times. The tears were from my heart. The scene at the cemetery was different. Now I was watching my youngest son being lowered into the earth. Dirt would soon be his blanket. Grass his coverlet. This wasn't supposed to be. I grabbed Eric's hand. He squeezed mine back. His tears had become almost as constant as mine. Eric had a serious case of older brother syndrome. To him it was his fault. He should have been able to protect his little brother. Advise him better on what was safe and what was not. Especially with me focusing on my next slug of vodka and his mother God knew where. He had been told that it was his job to keep an eye on Josh since he was old enough to understand. "Eric! Watch out for Josh!" "Eric...take care of your little brother." "Eric, where's Josh?" Now ever since I got back from Wisconsin when I stared down into his face he could not look up at me. Following my endless trip back home, when I walked down the jet-way back into the RDU International airport and saw him standing there with his back to the gate I walked up to him and put my hand on his shoulder. He did not look into my face. He just turned and buried his tear-streaked face into my shoulder and said, "I'm sorry Dad. This was all my fault." I clutched his head and said, "Come on son. Let's go home." We talked little during the days preceding the funeral, but now here we were. Clasping our hands. No one else in the world but us. We got through the wake. We had decided to have it at the funeral home. The thought of our house holding all these friends and staying around to "make sure we were ok" was unbearable. The funeral home was the right spot for this event. It was not comfortable for Eric and I to stand up under the bright light of scrutiny while our friends passed on sincere condolences, but we helped to ease the pain of those around us. Even Mary came up and hugged me. Then she turned and tried to hug Eric. He cursed at her and walked away. I tried to explain that he was seriously hurting, but she didn't want to hear it. I began to say goodbye. She dropped one cold tear, looked for her new husband, and then she rescinded back into a nether world of denial. I once again confirmed in my head that she was gone. Maybe always had been. I caught up with Eric and we went home together not mentioning the incident with his mother. Six days after the funeral I walked downstairs to our kitchen, began to cook breakfast and thought about what to do next. I hadn't had a drink since leaving the American Club. I started to feel like a human being again. I had not heard, smelled or felt the presence of Granny since I had quit drinking. I started to wonder if her visits were real. Certainly I would have smelled that rosewater essence at the funeral. Over the preparation of scrambled eggs, bacon and cheese bisquits I mulled over a plan I had been working out. Half way through my cooking Eric walked into the kitchen. "How you doin' bud." I asked. He sat down in the bar part of the kitchen and said, "fine." I looked at him, dished a plate of steaming hot breakfast out onto his plate and said, "I want you to do me a favor today...Okay?" He spooned some jelly onto his toast and said, "Yeah...sure...no problem." He didn't ask what. He didn't have any real tone to his voice anymore. He just sat there and ate. An hour later we were driving up to our country club just outside of Raleigh. Eric looked over at me and said, "What are we doing here?" I pulled the car into one of the slots close to the clubhouse and said, "Eric, did you ever notice that life is a lot like golf and golf courses?" He scowled, shook his head and started to say something. "No...don't talk...just listen for one minute. Your Great Granny...God rest her soul, has been talking to me over the past few weeks. At first, I thought I was hallucinating. Maybe because I was drinking too much. Maybe because I was under too much stress." I put my head down into my hands and said, "It really doesn't matter how I have heard her. The fact is I have. Or...I did. I haven't heard anything lately. And Eric, I swear to God she has made sense. She tried to warn me about Josh. She tried to get me to open up to you and to your brother. She told me to cherish the time we had together and work through any rough spots we had already had just like playing a tough round of golf. I sloughed her off. She told me to connect with you. I pushed her off again." I walked back to the trunk and popped the lid. I reached down into the trunk and pulled out my golf spikes. "All my life my Granny, your Great-Granny has been trying to guide me. Push me along life's path with golf. But I refused to listen. I refused to hear what she was saying. But Eric...good God Eric, she was talking to my heart the whole time." I put my feet on the ground, looked straight up into the clear blue

Carolina air and said, "Now it's time for you and I to connect. I hope we can do it through golf." I tossed a new pair of Foot-Joy golf shoes to Eric, smiled, and said, "Let's go play."

Fifty-two

We began to play that day, almost two years ago now, and built a relationship that was grounded in the love between a father and a son, and a respect for a game played by men and women who respect the challenges the game had to offer. We both applied the lessons Granny had passed on to me all those years ago back at Northridge Country Club in Granville Falls. We both had pulled our lives together and began to succeed not only in our working lives, mine at QI and Eric's at N.C. State, but at golf. My handicap hovered in the low single digits while Eric, who had always had solid athletic prowess, played to scratch. Towards the second anniversary of Josh's death Eric came to me with a sincere request of his own. I was sitting in our den reading a business plan for a new bio testing facility when he walked in and said, "Dad, I think you and I should play in the North Carolina Father/Son Championship down at Pinehurst next week." I looked up from my work and laughed, "Yeah sure!" I said in my best Norwegian accent. "Vat makes you tink ve could efen qualify for dat?" "Come on Dad, I'm serious. We could do it. As a matter of fact I already sent in the application and it came back today." I was shocked, but in a very pleasant way. Eric shot me a wide grin and shouted, "We're in!"

Pinehurst No. 2

I looked over the top of the low clubhouse nestled not too far from the eighteenth green of No. 2 and took in a deep breath. The statues of Donald Ross and his friend the former president of Pinehurst C.C. Richard Tufts, father of amateur golf, posed gazing at the frozen form of U.S. Open Champion Payne Stewart locked in a victory shout. Three ghosts, locked in bronze watching over the greatest golf course on the planet. I felt great. Eric stood about ten feet away polishing his Scotty Cameron putter with an oilcloth. He was frowning just a bit. I walked over to him, put my sinewy tired arm around his shoulder and said, "Thanks."

"Thanks for what Dad?" He tried to pull away. "I blew it for us. We could have won if I hadn't gotten greedy and tried to swing out of my shoes."

I rubbed his shoulder and said, "Hey, we're not one hundred per cent out of it yet. There are still others out there who can fall back. Besides, no matter what happens this was one of the greatest days of my life. I'm proud of you Eric. You played like a champ."

"But I broke one of Granny's strictest rules. Right when we needed it the most I seized up. Tried to go for it all. I suck!" My forearm gently spun Eric face to face with me. I looked him square in his dark blue eyes...held them in my gaze for a moment, and then pulled him close toward me. I hugged him as hard as I could with as much love as I could muster. And though my words were a bit thick I told him this: "We've been through a lot champ. No one ever said it was going to be easy, and we've both made mistakes, but we've both made good choices too. I hate that my marriage went sour. I will always miss the times I did not spend with you and with Josh. I will always feel some responsibility for him not being here with us right now. But let's focus on what we have done in the last two years. What we are going to do in the future. And let's never forget what we have done together right here, right now, in this very special place." This was the best way possible to spend the anniversary of your brother's passing. And it was your idea." I looked up at the heavens briefly trying to hold back a gush of tears. "I love you Eric. We are a team, now and forever." A tear rolled down Eric's cheek.

"I love you too Dad. Thanks for being here. Let's go home"

We hugged each other tight for a moment longer, let go and then walked off the most famous finishing hole in the world. The one we finished together. Watching us move toward our future were the bronze glistening eyes of Mr. Ross, Mr. Tufts, U.S. Open Champion Payne Stewart and those of two shimmering images standing close to the three bronzed statues. Granny twirled her hickory putter, gave out a short cackle, grabbed Josh by the ear and said, "Come on kid...we're done here. I got stories to tell you, lessons to give you and some great new courses to show you. Let's git movin'."

About the Author

Richard J. Domann has spent the last twenty-three years working in the pharmaceutical industry focusing on sales, marketing, government, trade relations and operations. The opportunity to link his love of golf to his business career has provided a foundation for his writing. Richard is a member of the North Carolina Writer's Network.

Printed in the United States
1488500001B/138

9 781414 006307